Taunting

Cyborg Seduction - Book Seven

By Laurann Dohner

Taunting Krell

by Laurann Dohner

Krell hates humans. They left him scarred and undesirable to females. He's lived a lonely existence in his home world because of their brutality. So he's angry when he's ordered to interrogate the captured human. She's the enemy, a soldier from Earth. He'll show her the same mercy they showed him. None.

Cyan didn't expect to survive her mission against the Markus Models but she's stunned and elated to be confronted by cyborgs. The past and present collide, however, when she sees Krell. He's part of a dangerous secret from another life — and he's also completely irresistible.

Krell is certain Cyan can't be trusted. He's determined to keep her at a distance...but Cyan is just as determined to get the big, sexy cyborg into her bed.

Dedication:

A special thanks to Mr. Laurann for being my hero. I'd also like to thank Kele Moon for reading everything I write and always being honest. Here's to new beginnings when you really need a fresh start in life.

Cyborg Seduction Series

Taunting Krell

Copyright © August 2016

Editor: Kelli Collins

Cover Art: Dar Albert

ISBN: 978-1-944526-74-0

Prologue

The distant past on Earth
Cyborg Detention Center

Emily heard the door softly open and flicked her wrist. The screen on her computer instantly changed to display a card game. She glanced at the smaller monitor to her right and relaxed. A smile curved her lips while she watched the tall cyborg approach from behind.

Mavo's masculinity flooded her as she breathed him in. There was something to be said about overdeveloped senses. He'd showered recently, he'd used the musky new soap she'd ordered for him, and she closed her eyes to savor how good it blended with his natural scent. Her eyes opened.

"What are you doing here?" She waited for him to move within her side vision as he crouched next to her chair. She stared into his beautiful green eyes. They always took her breath away when she gazed into them. The color complemented his pale, silvery skin and jet-black hair. "We said our goodbyes earlier."

He didn't smile back. "Come with us."

Sadness gripped her hard. She forced back tears that instantly formed. "Don't make our last conversation be an argument. We've been over this a thousand times."

"I won't leave without you." His strong jawline tensed and his full lips pressed tightly together. "I'll carry you."

She wished it were that simple. "And then what?"

"We'll make it work."

Her wrist flicked again, her original screen returned, and she glanced at it. The small sensor on her forehead vibrated as it read her brainwaves—her thoughts—and she watched what she was doing instead of continuing to stare at him.

"You need to go. Time is running out."

From the corner of her eye, she saw him turn his head to peer at the screen.

"What is this?"

"I'm reprogramming the satellites. You'll have a better chance if the surface can't warn the ships what is going on down here. It will fool them into believing there have been some solar flares. It's going to take effect in ten minutes. It's going to really screw up communications. It will give you about a fifteen-minute window. I couldn't give you more time without creating suspicion."

"Emily," he growled her name, "you've done more than enough and risked too much already for us. Get out of there before they realize you've hacked it."

"That's the awesome thing about being me. I am good at this shit. My entire life revolves around computers. They haven't tracked me yet. I sneaked inside to get you the override codes for all the ships orbiting Earth. I changed the delivery schedules to put more shuttles on the ground." Her wrist flicked again to open a third screen. "I reinstated your people to make sure no alarms will go off when you pass through the atmosphere. The crews aboard the ships orbiting above will read you as actively on duty. They'll believe you're just coming to report for work."

"Emily." His hand reached up to brush her cheek. "Stop. You risk your life every time you do this."

What life? She held that thought back, not speaking it aloud. She met his gaze, saw the sadness there, and wished she could touch him back but she had too much to do. His warm thumb caressed her skin, pleasure at that slight contact was something she'd come to appreciate.

"What are they going to do to me? Unhook me from the system?" She couldn't prevent the snort. "My father is God to them. He created your people and is responsible for those androids they depend upon so much. They wouldn't dare risk alienating him by arresting me. I'm all he loves besides his work."

The green of his eyes darkened with anger. "Come with me. Please?"

Longing gripped her so strongly that she had to look away for fear he'd see it. "I can't. Eighty percent of my body doesn't work. I'd only be a burden."

"Never," he rasped.

Emily had to fight back more tears before she dared meet his intense gaze again. "We're doing this to give you the opportunity to have a normal life. You and your people deserve to be free and happy. You wouldn't have that with me tagging along."

His jaw clenched again. "You want me happy? Allow me to unplug you and carry you out of here with us. Do you think I won't take care of you?"

She knew without question that he would. There lay the problem. "I love you, my friend. In a way, we're family since we are both creations of the same man, in one way or another."

"I love you too. I don't want to leave you behind."

"That's why I'm saying no. You've taken such good care of me in the past year that you've been assigned as my guard. All my other guards avoided me, stayed as far from me as they could, but you became my friend. We talk and what you've given me is more than you'll ever know. I don't want you to spend whatever time I have left doing the things the nurses do." She lifted her chin. "Changing my diapers and feeding me is not a chore you should ever suffer." It embarrassed her to even admit it to him. "I require too much care."

"I'd do it happily. Please," he rasped. "Allow me take you with us."

"Stop!" She knew she'd start to cry if he didn't. She wanted to go with the cyborgs so bad it hurt. "No. Stop arguing with me. We've done this too many times. Resources are going to be limited, you don't even know where to go once you're free and the last thing you need is someone being an extra hindrance."

"No one would dare say that."

Of course not. Mavo would kick their asses. She remembered the human guard Mavo had beaten up two months before for making a joke about her physical handicaps. The price for defending her had been two days detained within a holding cell until she'd been able to make her father pull strings to return him to duty as her guard. She'd had to beg and tell her father what the offensive guard had said to get her cyborg released. Her

10

father had wanted her protected and that's what Mavo had done. Being punished for following orders had been wrong.

"I know." She glanced at the time. "You have to go. You know where you need to be in eight minutes."

His thumb stopped moving. "I'm taking you. I won't leave you behind. I just can't. We owe you too much to abandon you. They may punish you if they discover what you've done."

"No." Her voice shook. "Don't. I'll slow you down."

"I don't care. I'll stay if you won't go."

"No!" She jerked her arm and managed to bump her hand against his side. "Don't you dare, Mavo. I told you I intercepted the government notes of their last meeting. They are planning to scrap the program. They'll kill all of you."

"I'd rather die than abandon you."

Sincerity shone in his eyes. It made her want to cry again and love him even more, if that were possible. He meant so much to her, even if he didn't see her the way she did him. He felt gratitude, protective, but never viewed her as a sexually attractive woman.

"You promised me you'd go. You swore."

"You made me." His voice deepened with anger. "You can be irritated with me later, once we leave Earth." He paused. "Together." His hand dropped away and he turned in his crouched position to reach for her wrist.

"Don't!"

A pop sounded and her link to the computer severed when he disconnected her.

"Damn it, Mavo. Stop. I know you're worried about what will happen to me but I won't survive a week if I leave Earth. My time is short enough, maybe a year at most before my body calls it quits, but I'll take every day I can get. I swear I'll be fine. They won't arrest me. At worst they'll box my computer access to prevent me from connecting to any other exterior sources. My father won't allow them to arrest me and they need him too much to mess with him. He always gets what he wants."

He hesitated. "I'll worry."

She stared into his eyes. "I know, but don't. I'm a big girl, I knew what I was doing, and my father will protect me once you're gone." She decided to distract him. "Is everyone excited? You have to think about them. They need you more than I do."

His head bowed. "Yes. They can't wait to leave here." His tormented gaze rose. "Are you sure you don't want to come with us?"

"Hook me back in. I want to monitor it going down and do what I can to help you guys escape."

She breathed easier once he reconnected her to the machines, relieved she'd been able to talk sense into him, and glanced at her screen. She focused on a small, red blinking alert.

"Oh no. Security has grabbed one of your people." She pulled up the report. "It's a male, he's been taken to security building two, and they plan to kill him. They believe he knows of some plot to escape." Her heart raced. "There's four guards with him, according to what I'm reading." She focused

12

her mind and pulled up the security cameras inside the detention center, found the one where the cyborg male had been taken, and activated the live feed.

Four guards had a cyborg male on his knees, his hands restrained behind his back, while they kicked and beat him. One of the bastards held a knife, slashing at the man, and horror filled Emily. She couldn't see much of the cyborg with the guards surrounding him but she could see flashes of red from how much they'd already made him bleed. She opened another screen with the cyborg's file, revealing a picture of him.

"I don't know him. Do you?"

"Yes," Mavo snarled. "He's a friend."

"Go save him," she ordered as she hacked into the mainframe of the detention center. "The attack will begin soon so hurry. Get to him. I'll unlock the exterior doors and trigger the fire alarms to prevent them from killing him. They'll exit the south side the way they've been trained to do in the fire drills. They'll just leave him inside the cell to burn to death. God, I hate those jerks. He's helpless. You're going to have to run. The first distraction begins in four minutes."

A hand brushed her cheek. Emily peered up at Mavo. "Thank you. I'll never forget you or how you helped us."

"Be happy. That's thanks enough. Now go!"

He rose to his impressive height and spun away, leaving her alone. She glanced at the monitor to watch his back disappear. Sadness gripped her for a moment, until her focus returned to the poor captured cyborg inside the detention cell. She triggered the fire alarms in the building and groaned when the guards backed away from their prey.

The cyborg slumped to the floor. As the jerks ambled for the exit, she realized just how bloodied the silvery pale skin of their victim had become. Tears blinded her. She had discovered him too late. No one could survive that kind of blood loss. She could see it pooling on the concrete floor around his body, sprawled motionless where he'd fallen. Her gaze drifted to his file, his photo—a handsome male with deep blue eyes and jet-black hair. That face would haunt her, she'd remember the cyborg she'd failed to save, and her heart broke a little.

Anger gripped her next. On the cameras, she followed the guards' progress until they reached the outside. She activated the auto locks on that side of the building to prevent them from returning. They didn't try, too busy congratulating each other with grins and man-pats over the cruelty they'd just dealt out to a cyborg.

Motion drew Emily's gaze to one of the camera views. Mavo rushed into the room, to the downed cyborg, scooped him up into his strong arms and ran for the doors. The cyborg he held didn't appear to be alive.

A sudden explosion pierced the quiet around her, her chair and everything on her desk shook from the shockwave, and a loud siren blared throughout the compound that housed the cyborg prisoners. Emily focused on her screen. She had work to do, no time for emotion, and she started to lock down sections of the facility to trap the human employees inside the buildings. It would prevent them from helping security when they attempted to stop the cyborgs.

Time lost meaning. She barely took notice of the following explosions, more than aware of how many would come. None had been set near her office so she wouldn't be injured accidentally. The cyborgs hadn't wanted her hurt during their escape. She locked down the main gates to prevent any outside interference, shut down all interior communications to confuse security, and sent out an automated warning for the shuttle pilots on the ground to rush to safety inside the break room she unlocked to allow them admittance. She smiled while watching them abandon their shuttles. She sealed those doors once the last pilot entered the building. They wouldn't be able to return to their posts.

She barely took note when large groups of cyborgs rushed out onto the tarmacs to fill the shuttles. She didn't have time to appreciate that wonderful sight. Someone tried to hack into the system to lock her out.

"Shit." *They know I'm here but it doesn't matter.* She pushed back her thoughts, concentrating instead on preventing them from gaining control. They'd try to access the automatic weapons. No way would she allow that to happen. "You're good, fellow hacker," she muttered. "But I'm better."

A popping noise sounded behind her, someone blowing the lock she'd sealed, and the door to her office suddenly opened hard enough to slam loudly into the wall. Her gaze flickered to the monitor that revealed the camera feed trained behind her back. Two security officers rushed inside.

"Stop what you're doing," one of them demanded. "Turn off your computers."

She ignored them, initiating a reboot of the system that would keep everyone, including her, from being able to use the auto systems for at least

15

three minutes to give the cyborgs more time and ordered it to launch before a loud noise gave her a start.

Red splattered her main screen. She stared at it, uncomprehending for two blinks of her eyes. *Blood.* Her chin lowered until she could see her chest. Bright, wet red soaked her shirt, ran into her lap, and she licked her lips.

"You shot me."

A rough hand grabbed her shoulder and her body was thrown from her chair to the floor. Pain, as much as the shock from what they'd done, nearly made her pass out. *They really shot me.* She opened her eyes and glanced at her monitors. She couldn't see all of them but caught enough of one to see it scrolling codes. A smile curved her lips. She'd triggered the reboot of the system. The hacker would be locked out.

"Did you stop her?" a loud voice boomed. "Fuck! You shot her? Shit! Get a medic. What the hell were you thinking? I told you to stop her, not kill her. Goddamn it! Move! Get a medic! We can't let her die. Her father will have our asses."

Craig Summers, the head of security, dropped to his knees next to Emily. His big hand gripped her jaw to force her to peer up at him. "Why did you do it? Goddamn it, Emily. Your father is going to go insane when he finds out you helped them escape. I knew it had to be you. No one else can break through our security measures."

Breathing hurt. She dragged in air, found it tough to do and understood the bullet must have pierced a lung when the taste of blood filled her mouth. She cleared her throat.

"Did they get all the shuttles away?"

Anger, and finally sadness, filled the older man's pale-green eyes. She'd known Craig most of her life. He and her father were friends. "Yeah, baby. They did. Not that it's going to help them. When they reach space the ships up there are going to blow them to kingdom come."

She chuckled, coughed, and choked on blood. "No."

His hand tightened on her face. "You made sure of that, didn't you? What were you thinking? They are dangerous. They are going to attack Earth, kill us all, and you made it possible."

"Emily!" her father's panicked voice yelled. "Oh my God. What did you do?"

Craig released her, moved out of the way and rose to his feet. "I didn't shoot her, Edward. I swear. Two of the guys did it. I'm so sorry. It's terminal."

Her eyes closed. She choked on blood, knew she wasn't going to survive, but the cyborgs had made it off the surface. A sense of peace filled her. She'd finally done one wonderful, meaningful thing with the short life she'd been given.

* * * * *

"Stay with me, Emily Rose," a familiar voice demanded.

Her eyes opened and she stared in confusion at her father's face inches above her own. He looked haggard, his normally neat white hair messed up as if he'd teased it, and she realized they were inside his lab when she took note of the ceiling above his head. It confused her to still be

17

alive. She knew she'd been shot. With her sick, weakened body, it shouldn't be possible for her to have made it from the floor of her office to his lab two buildings away.

"Hurry up," he yelled at someone, turning his face away. "We're losing her again. I don't know if I can revive her a third time."

"This isn't going to work," a female voice sobbed, one Emily recognized as her father's longtime assistant, Bella. "Her heart is damaged, both lungs, and I think we fractured her spine when we just scooped her up and ran with her, Eddie."

"It can work." Her father's voice broke and he leaned over Emily. "Stay with me. Just a few minutes more, sweetie. I've been working on a project for the past three years just for you. I knew your body would fail eventually and I don't want to lose you."

"Damn it, this is insane. It's just a theory that it could work, not something we've ever tried, and we're not gods. We thought we had more time before she'd start to die. We're not ready!" The male voice hissed the warning.

"She's out of time." Her father ran his fingers through her hair to rub her scalp. His tears dampened her face where they fell on her cheeks. "We've got nothing to lose at this point. We can work the kinks out later but we need to save her first. Just do it. Is the prototype ready?"

Doctor Percy Olson, her father's longtime friend and research assistant, suddenly hovered over Emily. He met her gaze and she saw fear on his aged features, regret. "Yeah. It's out. This is going to hurt her a lot."

"Do it," her father sobbed. "She's lost to us for certain if we don't try."

18

She'd grown up with Percy. He was like an uncle to her. His daughter happened to be her best friend. She saw tears swim in his eyes before he looked away. Something hot and agonizing pieced her skull.

She screamed and fell into nothingness.

Chapter One

Present time, decades later

"Systems check," Cyan ordered the computer.

"Everything is fine," it responded.

Frustration rose. "Then why aren't you responding the way you should?"

"Perhaps it is an operator failure on your end."

"Damn hunk of junk," she muttered under her breath. "I'm fine."

"You could have made an error."

She flipped it off. "Just keep your heading. How long until we reach Belta Station?"

"Ten minutes."

Cyan checked the readings. No ships were within range, a good thing in her mind, but the Markus Models she tracked were smart. Anger stirred. Why she'd been sent on the mission wasn't a mystery. She'd made an enemy of General Vargus after she'd broken his thumb for grabbing her ass.

"This is a suicide mission if we find them."

"Response noted."

"Note this, you hunk of junk." She kicked the side of the pilot's station with her boot. "What happened to the signal? You're supposed to keep tracking it. It was there but now it just disappeared?"

"Affirmative."

"Maybe those stationers managed to kill all those androids. That would be too tidy, wouldn't it?"

"Response noted."

"Have I mentioned I hate when you say that whenever you don't know how to respond? And don't say it again. I'm talking to myself so butt out while I have a decent conversation for once."

The computer remained silent. Cyan rose from her chair, her fingers absently rubbing the weapon strapped to her thigh, and paced the floor. "It's got to be a trap."

She paused and reached for one of the cabinets but cursed. "I hate being short." She had to find something to stand on to reach it, tore it open, withdrew spare energy shots for the gun and shoved them inside a pocket of her pants. "I swear that dickhead assigned me to this shuttle on purpose. He could have let me have the *Derik* but no. He stuck me on the *Blarney* where everything is higher. What a prick!"

"Belta Station within docking range. Hailing." The computer paused. "No response. I read extensive damage. They have hull breaches on two levels."

"Of course they do. They were attacked by those crazy defense Markus Models that are one circuit short of mass murder."

"Response noted."

Cyan screamed in frustration. It made her feel slightly better. She'd had to spend nearly two weeks alone inside the ancient shuttle with only the computer for company. General Vargus wanted her to suffer for embarrassing him in front of his men when she'd openly rejected his advances. The fact that she'd actually broken a bone hadn't helped. No other soldier had ever been sent on a dangerous solo mission.

"I'm just special," she snorted. "He's got no idea."

"Response noted."

Her weapon cleared the holster before she realized she'd aimed it at the computer module. Her finger froze over the trigger and she took deep breaths. "Blowing you to pieces may feel good but it would only make my job harder. Stop talking. That's an order. Silence."

She planted her butt on the seat, took the controls and did a visual inspection of the large space station that had sent out a distress signal weeks prior. They'd been under heavy attack, had identified the Markus Models as the aggressors, and she'd been sent to investigate.

The station had put up a vicious fight. They'd taken a lot of damage and obviously hadn't just surrendered. She glanced down.

"Computer? Why aren't you scanning for life signs?"

"There is too much interference from debris. I'm unable to get accurate findings to display."

"Great. I guess when I board Belta Station I'll just hope I don't run in to any surprises. My birthday is coming up and here I thought I wouldn't get anything."

"Response—"

"Noted!" Cyan yelled. "Yeah. Shut up. I am ordering you to stop saying that."

"I'm unable to follow that order."

"I hope I run into one of those crazy-ass androids. I'd love to kill something at this point." She steered the shuttle against one of the undamaged docking doors. She turned off the engines and stood.

"Wish me luck."

"Good luck."

Cyan moved quickly through the shuttle. She'd usually have a team of at least eight soldiers under her command to board the station with her. No help waited when she entered the cargo bay. She paused at the door, grabbed one of the masks off the wall, and shoved it over her face. She ignored the tug on her long hair. The general would have a fit if he knew she'd stopped braiding it against her skull. It was against regulation to wear it down while on duty but it was also against regulation to send a soldier on a mission without an armed team to back her up.

One glance at the monitor indicated the pressure on the other side of the door was stable enough to enter the station. She gripped her weapon and her other hand keyed in the code to unlock the door. Air hissed when the seal broke and the door popped. She used her foot to kick it open. She wondered if the area of the station she was about to enter had been depressurized since the attack and if her docking had auto-triggered the onboard computer to pressurize the area. It would be a very short trip if that were the case since she'd be contained in a small area before hitting sealed doors.

"I hate old shuttles," she muttered but knew it had been the only smart thing the general had insisted upon. The Markus androids could remote hack computers. On the older ships everything was pretty much manual and the onboard computer was only voice activated from the same room in which the module had been installed. They traveled through space slower but once in range of the station, they couldn't be controlled by one of those freaky Markus Models if they'd taken it over.

Destruction and death met her the moment she walked onto the station. Two dead bodies lay decaying on the floor. She curled her lip, grateful for the mask that kept her from smelling what had to be putrid air. Their severe decomposition assured her that this part of the station hadn't been affected at all by the hull breaches from the attack. Only being exposed to high levels of oxygen could do that to a body in space. She could remove the mask but didn't do it.

She entered one of the corridors. More bodies were piled up as if someone or something had chased them, shot them in the back, and they'd tripped over the fallen bodies to collapse on top of each other. She counted twelve dead stationers. It was hard to tell if they had been male or female but they were wearing civilian shoes when they'd died. One body looked suspiciously small.

"Oh no," she muttered, distraught. "They had kids here. It's too close to deep space and pirates. What were you thinking?"

No one answered but she didn't expect it. She stepped over some of the bodies, moved slowly, and continued deeper into the station. She kept alert. It was likely the Markus Models had figured out how to mask their tracking signals. They had a scary ability to adapt. She'd been fully briefed on them after they'd been created and the trouble had started. Her vote would have been to pass on that project if anyone had asked her before they decided to make the defective things.

The defense androids were nearly indestructible except by electrocution. They were also self-aware, had escaped from the manufacturing facility where they'd been undergoing testing, and were extremely dangerous to anything living.

Her grip on her weapon tightened and her left hand reached for the other weapon at her waist. All she had to do was pierce their skin with a bullet and shoot energy shots at them to jolt them with electricity and take them down. Her ears strained to pick up any sound but only eerie silence greeted her.

"Not having a good feeling about this," she whispered, the sound of her voice comforting. "Every living person on this station is dead. I just know it."

She'd hoped to find some survivors on Belta Station. Sure, they hadn't responded to hails since the initial distress signals but she'd still been optimistic that it was a case of their communications being taken out. Cyan tried not to stare at the bodies she passed. It freaked her out a lot and depression settled in deep with all the death surrounding her. There had been thirty-nine souls aboard according to the manifesto, all civilians, and obviously some of them had been children.

She paused at the sealed-down section when she came to it. The door indicators blinking red in warning told her she'd found the breached section of the station. She knew she could override the safety procedures to attempt to pressurize the affected areas but there wasn't any reason to do it. No survivors would have made it without air. Even if they'd managed to lock down inside a secured room with a sealed door, two weeks would have killed them. No food, no water and a breached section stopped sending oxygen to the affected areas. They would have suffocated before they starved.

She located the main control room. She really wished she hadn't as her gaze slowly took in over ten bodies. Weapons fire scarred the walls, dried, black bloodstains smeared on parts of the metal floor and she knew this had been where the stationers had made their last stand. One body drew her attention.

She aimed her gun at it and tread carefully, ready to shoot the hell out of it if it moved. It was male, had brown hair and wasn't a mess of disgusted death rot. Her heart accelerated. It had the exact size and shape of a Markus Model. Their hair and eye color could be changed out, along with their voices, but not their general size or cloned faces. It remained sprawled facedown. Her boot nudged it.

She nearly screamed from fright when it jerked, barely trapped the sound inside her throat, and hissed instead. She leapt back to put at least four feet between them. Its fingers clawed against the floor but it didn't move anything else.

"Great."

The head tried to turn but it just twitched. It took her long seconds to take a few calming breaths before she approached. One good kick and she jumped back again. The kick flipped it onto his back. She studied it.

"Wow!" The Markus Model's eyes were open but it didn't attack. Burn marks scorched his chest and neck pretty badly. "They fried you, didn't they? Just not enough to totally take you out."

One of his hands twitched. She saw a cable lying about three feet to his left along with the decaying body of a stationer, who still gripped it. A shudder ran through her. The stationer had obviously torn lose a live electrical connection once attached to the control panel to attack the Markus Model. He'd shoved the live current against the downed android and they'd both fried in the process.

Cyan crouched, cocked her head and peered at the android. "Can you talk?"

His mouth parted. "Help me."

"Oh I plan to. Where are your brothers?"

He paused. "They aren't here."

Good to know, she thought. "Where are they? I'll tell them you're still functioning and have them come get you. I'm not good at fixing stuff," she lied.

"I am uncertain. I have no linking capabilities. I have come to the conclusion they believed I terminated when the link between us severed. They have not returned."

"How many of them are there?"

"We are eight Models."

She hid her grimace. Two would be difficult but seven still on their feet were bad odds to face off against. "Why did you attack the station?"

27

He paused and she could have sworn his eyes actually sparked. "Information unobtainable. I am suffering connection problems to memory and functions."

"Poor baby." He watched her. She sighed. "Did any of the humans survive?"

"Affirmative."

Surprise jolted her. "How many?"

"One female."

Cyan turned her head and studied the room before looking back at him. "Where is she? Do you know?"

"She left the station eight cycles previous."

"How?"

"A shuttle docked and retrieved her."

"Do you know which shuttle? Who it was?"

"Negative. I am unable to link to the station computer."

"How do you know she left on a shuttle?"

"The onboard computer verbally warned of a shuttle approach and I heard voices. The female screamed and I heard a male say he had her. They undocked."

"Well, that information wasn't very helpful. Now I've got to try to track her down. I don't suppose you know if they were pirates?" Cyan really hoped not or there wouldn't be a reason to try to locate the survivor. Eight days with pirates would have made her either completely insane or very dead.

"Negative."

"Okay, well, thanks for playing." She straightened to her feet. "I'm going to help you now."

"Good."

She didn't bother to shoot him and waste bullets. His open chest wounds gave her access. She pointed the energy gun at him and fired two shots. One would have done it but she wanted to make sure the stationer hadn't wasted his life when he'd attempted to kill the Markus Model. This time she'd make certain it permanently shut down.

The body jerked and smoke rose. The report of her weapon sounded unusually loud inside the otherwise silent control room. She watched as the eyes turned white, the mouth dropped open, and it totally ceased functioning.

"Oh, just for shits and giggles." She fired one more energy shot into the thing. "Better to be safe than sorry. I hope you keep burning in computer hell for killing all those people."

Cyan walked over to the monitoring station that still appeared operational while she holstered her weapons. She paused but then frowned. Two docking doors registered in use. The *Blarney* accounted for one. The survivor would have used the same door to flee if another ship had been docked when the attack happened.

The color drained from her face at the implication. "Computer, emergency response," she whispered to override most of its protocols. "State the times when the docking locations were activated."

The computer responded. "Twenty-three minutes and forty seconds." It paused. "Ten minutes and nineteen seconds."

Cyan spun, her weapons clearing their holsters, gripped in each hand, and her heart raced. Someone had docked after she had. She wasn't alone on the station anymore. She swallowed hard. She'd found one Markus, which meant at least seven more androids were unaccounted for. She had a really bad feeling that she'd just found them or worse, they'd found her.

"Either way, I'm so screwed," she whispered. She needed to return to her shuttle if they hadn't already entered it. She cursed the age of the *Blarney* again. No way would she be able to outrun one of the newer shuttles the androids had stolen when they'd fled Earth. She rubbed her leg, the energy shots a bumpy mass inside her pocket, to assure herself she wouldn't run out if it came down to a battle. Dread twisted inside her belly, knowing she'd have to retrace her steps to reach her shuttle.

She eased into the main hall, kept close to the wall, and her gaze darted around, watching for any sign of movement. She inspected each body on the floor before she passed it. She didn't want one to rise up—an android using the dead to fool her—and continued to head for the section her shuttle had docked to. Hope flared that she might make it out of this mess alive.

She reached the final corridor and glanced around the corner where her shuttle awaited. One look made her teeth clench. The door to her shuttle was closed. She'd left it open.

Screwed, she mouthed silently.

Scenarios formed inside her mind. They were either waiting on her shuttle to kill her there or they'd sealed it from the outside to trap her when she tried to enter. She glanced behind her to make sure nothing sneaked up. The corridor remained clear of movement.

She took deep breaths, hated the way her mask fogged under her nose, and knew she had to do something. She peeked around the corner again. Large crates were stacked near the far wall. They could be hiding behind them.

She glanced back and knew she was trapped either way. They could come at her from both directions if they'd split up. She decided to do something nuts. *It might work.* She knew they'd tried to negotiate with Earth Government to have their line of android Models released. They called each other brothers, as if that made them more real.

"Earth Government sent me," she called out loudly. "We want to negotiate."

Silence greeted that statement. "I'm their ambassador," she lied. "That's why I came alone if you checked my shuttle. I'm here to talk about settling our differences peacefully." She paused, trying to think up something they might want to hear. General Vargus would have a heart attack if he knew she'd stated this bullshit but he'd sent her on the mission alone. She wanted to save her own ass since he'd been determined to get her killed. "I have the authority to make a deal with you."

They didn't respond. *So much for that plan. It was crazy*, she admitted.

"Throw down your weapons," a deep male voice commanded. "We will negotiate."

31

She hesitated. "Okay. I'm just a woman. That's why they sent me. I'm only five foot three." For once it seemed a good thing she'd ended up so short. "I'm no threat," she lied.

It hurt her to toss her weapons. Both of them slid on the metal floor before she took a deep breath, blew it out and lifted her hands over her head. She made sure they could see her palms and spread fingers. She stepped out slowly, her gaze darting around the docking bay.

Two of them stood from behind the crates and the door to her shuttle opened. They'd been waiting in both places. She didn't even flinch when she heard boots strike the floor behind her. They'd even managed to creep up behind her. She'd had no chance whatsoever. She did frown as she stared at the full pressure suits they wore that shielded their faces with reflective glass. Markus Models wouldn't need space suits yet they wore them.

One of the men approached her and she knew she paled when she got a bead on his height. He wasn't just a hair under six feet tall the way Markus Models had been designed. He had to be six foot three, at least. She lowered her attention to his feet, hoping for a platform heel under his boots, but they seemed standard. She jerked her gaze to the tinted, mirrored shield covering his features. She saw her reflection staring back at her.

"Wow. I look pale, don't I?" She knew the humor would be lost on whoever they were but they weren't her missing Markus Models. She wasn't sure how much trouble she'd just landed in but whoever they were, it boded well for her. She could fight pirates hand to hand. "And this mask isn't too attractive, is it?"

The suited-up male stopped just short of walking into her. "You're from Earth Government?"

"Yes."

She'd already stated that and her assumption they were pirates grew. The uniform she wore should have told him she was a soldier if he was familiar with Earth. Most pirates had left the planet decades before to live on ships that leaked radiation and made them breathe stale recycled air. It mutated them in a matter of years. Insanity also ravaged their kind. She decided to speak slower since the guy had asked her what she'd already told them. His memory obviously wasn't good.

"You came to negotiate with us?"

"Sure." She forced a smile. Her clear mask showed her every facial expression and gave her a bit of a blurry view of what was going on behind her. She envied him the mirrored shield. "That's what I said. What are your demands? Do you want a puppy?"

He turned his head to glance at another suited-up person. The sound of boots on the deck stopped behind her. She had been aware that two of them flanked her. Five in all surrounded her. He looked back at her.

"A what?"

"A puppy. You know. They are cute little animals and are good company. Real loyal. Speaking of which, is this all of you? You didn't, by any chance, take the only survivor off the station, did you? Is she with you?"

"Perhaps the sight of the horror here has traumatized her," the guy from her shuttle muttered as he drew closer. "Or her mask is low on oxygen. The smells are too overpowering from the dead for her to have removed it. She could be suffering confusion from hypoxia." He paused. "You are the only female we found. We just arrived here."

The male who seemed to be in charge answered Cyan. "No, we don't want a puppy. What is your purpose here?"

She kept her smile in place while she glanced at the three in front of her. They weren't carrying weapons. That left the two behind her who could be armed. She didn't dare glance at them.

"Well, Belta Station sent out a distress signal and we knew how scary and super impressive you guys are. Earth wants to surrender to you. We give up. You win." Her body tensed. "We're waving a white flag."

The second the words were out, she blindly threw her leg back where she knew one of them stood—from the sound of their breathing—and plowed into the crotch of the suited man in a lucky estimation that he stood the same height as the others. Her hand shot forward when she kicked back, shoving hard at the guy in front of her. He stumbled, clearly caught off guard, and Cyan spun. She barely registered where the second man who'd been behind her was located before she leapt at him, did a roundhouse kick, and her booted heel connected hard with his chest. He roared out and flew backward.

Cyan dived for her weapons on the floor. Her fingers curled around the handles but a massive weight crushed down over her. The breath exploded

34

from her lungs as it was knocked out of her and two gloved hands tore at hers. The weapons were ripped away.

It shocked her that one of them had gotten the drop on her. They moved super fast to do that.

"Did you see that?" Another male voice gasped. "That was nearly beautiful. She's quick and effective."

"Tell that to Onyx. Are you well? It appears she didn't miss your scrotum."

Someone wheezed. "No. She did not. That hurts."

The crushing weight on top of her sighed. "She's an accurate fighter without even having to see her target. Earth is training humans much better these days."

He shifted enough for Cyan to breathe and her starved lungs appreciated it. She pushed suddenly, knocked him off her back and rolled away. She flipped to her feet and spun, her fists going up. She glared at the five men.

"I don't suppose you guys are into fair, are you? You know, just fight me one at a time?"

They stared at her silently. At least she assumed they did since all five masks faced her. She studied her reflection in their mirrored face shields. She looked small and not very threatening.

"You should have agreed to the puppy." She rolled her shoulder that ached from the heavy guy who'd nearly flattened her. "Now you're just going to have to settle for some serious ass whippings." She winked. "I'm kinky that way. I hope all of you are male because I am not into women."

35

"Is she serious? She wants to fight?" It was the guy she'd nailed in the nuts.

"I believe so." The one who'd crushed her onto the floor moments before spoke. "I am Ice and you do not want to do this. We don't wish to harm you. That's why we aren't drawing weapons. You may surrender without fear of death."

"So polite for a crazy nut job. I heard you pirates were whacked out of your heads. Kudos to you for remaining sane."

One of the men chuckled. "I like her."

"Did you understand what she said, Sky?" Ice's voice carried an annoyed tone.

"It's slang. She's congratulating us on not being insane." The guy moved a little to her left. "I am Sky and we're not pirates."

"Shit." Anger stirred. "Damn scavengers. I hate you assholes. I bet your mamas are so proud you grew up to go chase disasters just to make a buck. Now I won't feel sorry when I bloody the shit out of you. I'll even take you home to lock you up with pretty metals."

Sky chuckled. "She's adorable. She thinks we're criminals who illegally steal parts off ships that have sustained damage. She wants to arrest us."

Annoyance flashed fast and furiously inside Cyan. "So you aren't pirates, you're too tall and suited up to be crazy androids, and you aren't scavengers? Who are you?" She ran her gaze over their suits. "You sure aren't from the military. Those space suits were banned ten years ago, at least. They erode too easily in open space after a few hours and the seals sometimes blow at the neck joints from rapid decompression."

36

Their leader, Ice, took a menacing step toward her and she reacted. She reached for the small of her back, wrapped her fingers around the handle of the knife she kept there, and grabbed hold of his suit at the arm. She jerked hard, pulled him toward her with all her strength, and knocked him off balance. He crashed to the floor on his knees and she twisted to stand behind him. The knife ended up against his throat while she glared at his four pals.

"I'll decapitate him if any of you move."

"Shit," Sky gasped. "Who is she? She's strong and fast."

"Who are you?" She released the arm of her captive, certain the pressure of the knife at his throat would persuade the guy not to struggle and grabbed the connecter from the body of the space suit to his helmet. It popped loudly and she tore it over his head.

He'd be able to breathe but it sure wouldn't smell pretty with the decaying corpses. She looked down at his unusual hair, mostly white with gray streaks, and she tilted forward enough to get a glimpse of his face.

Shock made her gasp. She threw the knife down and released him. The helmet she held in her other hand crashed to the floor too. She backed up, nearly tripped over her own feet, and her entire world seemed to crash in on her stunned brain.

"Cyborgs," Cyan whispered.

The one on the floor bent forward, grabbed his helmet and turned his head to glare at her. He took a breath, his entire silvery-toned face contorted in disgust, and he coughed.

"She broke my helmet. The smell is unbearable." He staggered to his feet, put his arm up over the lower part of his face, and his blue eyes glared at her with fury. "I should rip your mask off."

Cyan sank to her knees, the fight gone out of her, and just stared at the tall man. Tears blinded her that she didn't bother to try to hold back. They slid down her cheeks freely.

She watched the cyborg's anger fade and confusion enter his gaze while he studied her. She sat on her legs, immobile, unable to look away from him.

"I think she's so terrified her mind has shut down," Sky softly rasped. "We don't kill women. Calm."

She turned her gaze to his face mask. "You survived. You're still alive."

Ice dropped his arm, breathed through his mouth and slowly approached. Cyan shifted her attention back to him. She didn't resist when he bent down, gripped her arm and pulled her to her feet.

"Resist again and I will fight back. I won't kill you but you will be hurt. We've held back so far but no more. You are obviously a soldier and not a harmless female."

"I'd never fight one of you." She sniffed. "You survived. You made it."

The cyborg had a totally baffled look on his face. "She is in shock. I need to get out of here. I can't take the smell."

"We'll take her home to interrogate her," the guy she'd kicked in the groin announced.

"Yes, we will, Onyx." Ice gripped her hard enough to bruise her arm but she barely registered that or where they took her.

"You survived." She said it to them as much as to herself.

"She's definitely in shock and has suffered mental trauma," one of the cyborgs sighed. "Are we so terrifying to humans that this is their reaction?"

Ice shrugged. "I assume so. At least she is being meek."

Cyborgs had somehow managed to survive in space. They weren't extinct as all the reports she'd read had stated. Cyan made a decision not to defend herself regardless of what they did to her. She refused to ever kill one of them.

Chapter Two

Onyx sat across from Cyan. Only two chairs had been placed inside the sterile room and one wall of glass showed her how shitty she looked. Her waist-length black hair hung in a mess around her body and her eyes were still a bit red from crying. She'd done more of that in the past seventeen hours than she had done in over a decade.

The cyborgs she'd surrendered to had flown her to the planet they'd settled on, and they'd taken her to some sort of holding area for prisoners. They'd built a real home, a city, and the glimpses she'd caught when they'd entered were impressive.

"What were you doing on Belta Station?" Onyx leaned closer to study her face carefully.

"Earth Government received their distress signal. They identified some escaped defense droids." She leaned back against her chair, crossed her ankles and rubbed her pants just for something to do. "They are called Markus Models. They believe they are sentient but they aren't. They have no compassion, no sense of right from wrong, and wouldn't hesitate to kill any living thing they come across."

"I wouldn't trust Earth Government's judgment on what is sentient or not."

Cyan watched him for a few long seconds. "Then trust me. They are ice cold inside. I met a few of them before I shipped out to track the escaped ones. Total metal heads. They appear human, thanks to biological body shells, but inside they are machines without souls. I wanted to see what I'd be dealing with when I was ordered to go on this mission. They scared the crap out of me."

"That's what Earth said about us."

"Cyborgs are the exception to the rule. They gave you basically human bodies for the most part, just genetically enhanced, and added cybernetics. These things are machines inside with fleshy exteriors."

Surprise widened his eyes. "You sound as if you're familiar with us."

"You could say that."

"Were you looking for us?"

"No." She shook her head. "I believed none of you had survived."

His dark gaze seemed to turn cold. "That's a lie."

"No. I'm not lying. I won't bullshit you."

He didn't appear convinced. "One of our kind recently escaped Earth. You want to pretend not to know this information?"

Shock reverberated through her. "No one told me that." She sat up a little straighter. "They kept one of you prisoner for all these years?"

He refused to answer.

Anger rose inside Cyan. "My father swore none of you remained on Earth. He lied to me? Is that what you're saying? I'd kick his ass if he wasn't already dead." She fumed.

"You wanted to kill us yourself?"

"No! I would have blown my cover and gotten them out."

"Your cover?"

She hesitated. "I can't talk about that."

"You will answer me."

"Some things aren't up for discussion. Is there anything else you want to know?"

He sighed. "I didn't want to do this but the interrogator will be called in if you don't cooperate."

"Scary shit, huh? Torture?" She winced. "I hate that." She glanced at her nails. "I just let them grow out too." Her gaze lifted to his. "Look, I stated I won't lie but I can't tell you some things about me. It's not that I don't want to but I just can't." She paused. "I've been conditioned."

"I don't understand."

"I spent three years having my head screwed with. Think of it as being brainwashed until I can't talk about what has been done to me without major migraines. I'm talking about ice-pick-to-the-head kind of pain. That's one thing that stuck. It makes me mad they did that but they wanted to make sure I could protect who I am. My father thought it was for the best. He had this God complex, always believed whatever he did was the right thing and I know in his heart he thought it was the only way to keep me breathing."

The cyborg stood. "You're trying to confuse me. It's the puppy game."

She grinned. "No, but I thought you were space pirates when I said that. I heard they are nuts. I was just trying to confuse you if you'd been one of those mutated freaks. I needed you off guard to attack. You're pretty smart to recognize what I was doing."

"I'm a cyborg."

42

"Right. Sorry. It's been a really long time since I've talked to one of you."

He advanced a threatening step forward. "When did you come into contact with a cyborg?"

Her mouth opened, she nearly told him the truth of who she was, but sudden pain jabbed her brain. She winced. "I can't tell you that. It was a long while ago."

He glared at the mirror wall. "Send him in. He'll make her talk."

Cyan wanted to curl into a ball. She really did hate torture but this would be extra hellish since she refused to fight back. Usually she'd kick someone's ass for putting a finger on her. In training she'd beaten on any instructor stupid enough to try hands-on techniques of how to resist torture. Her hands fisted. No matter what, she had to keep her cool.

The door opened and she knew her suffering would begin. She turned her head to check out the cyborg intent on making her scream "mercy". A tall gray-haired cyborg walked in. His hair made him appear older, the color of it aging him, but no wrinkles marred his handsome features. His strangely beautiful gaze held her attention captive. They were very pale blue with icy white specks in them and she wondered if he might be blind until they focused directly on her. He frowned.

"Look, sweetheart. I like you. You've got guts. Just tell Onyx everything he wants to know. You don't want to meet Krell. He's...cranky." The cyborg with the familiar voice sighed. "To put it mildly."

Onyx snorted. "That's being kind, Sky."

43

Sky glanced at the other male before looking back at Cyan. "He retired but the two males who usually interrogate prisoners are unavailable. One took time off after joining a family unit and the other one is cooling his heels inside a holding cell because he allowed his hatred for humans to make him screw up. Talk to me. When and where did you talk to another cyborg? Are cyborgs still being held in captivity on Earth?"

"As far as I know there aren't any cyborgs left in Earth Government's custody. I can assure you, if I had known about any of them, they wouldn't be there. I'd have helped them escape."

That seemed to shock the pale-eyed cyborg. "Why would you do that?"

"Would you believe me if I told you I'm pro-cyborg? I think what was done to your people had to be one of the biggest injustices in Earth's history."

"When did you speak to a cyborg? Where?" Sky took a threatening step toward her.

She tried to think of a way to answer without her brain seizing up. Anger at her father simmered yet again. He'd died just over a decade before but she still carried resentment over what he'd done to her. She had to forgive him overall though. He'd saved her and made her the way he had to keep her alive.

"It was a long time ago. Those cyborgs escaped Earth."

"I want a year, all the details, and where did they go?"

"I have no idea where they ended up. I thought they'd died until I ran into you on Belta Station."

"Year? Location on Earth?" Sky refused to give up.

She opened her mouth but another hot jab of pain sliced through her brain from even thinking about answering him when she realized she'd have to tell him who she once had been. "I can't."

The cyborg with the eerie yet beautiful eyes crouched before her but kept enough distance that he wasn't within kicking reach of her boots. "Give me the year and the circumstances. Were they prisoners? Where were they held? How did they escape?"

The pain grew worse and her stomach pitched as memories filled her head. She locked down her emotions and sealed her lips together. She couldn't answer. Some of the agony eased after she got control of the urge to blurt out the truth. Seconds ticked into minutes.

"Bring Krell in," Sky muttered toward the glass wall to whoever stood behind it. "Don't say I didn't warn you, sweetheart. I'm a lover, not a fighter. I can't stay here to watch this go down. It's against my nature to see someone hurt a woman." He straightened and met her gaze. "This is your last chance. Will you answer my questions?"

"I can't," she whispered honestly.

"Have it your way." He paused in front of the door that slid open then he disappeared around the corner.

Cyan braced for the worst. She'd never actually seen how they'd trained cyborgs when they'd been in captivity but she'd heard the rumors of what had been done to them. Some of the most brutal soldiers of Earth's Government had been instructors. Of course they mostly showed cyborgs how to torment someone by doing the same to them. The sound of boots

45

striking metal made her tense. Her attention focused on the open door. Whoever approached seemed angry by the way he stomped. The sound stopped.

"I don't want to do this." The harsh, raspy male voice terrified Cyan.

"Sorry, man," Sky answered, "it's not my call. She won't talk and she knows something about cyborgs. We need that information. She's refused to tell us when and where she had contact with our kind and we need dates to see if we can track them down. She's a soldier from Earth Government if it helps. You should have seen her fight. She looks fragile but she shoved Onyx's nuts into his stomach and took Ice to his knees and held a knife against his throat. She's probably one of the best fighters I've seen so watch your crotch and throat."

The scary voice growled. "Soldier? That helps. That means she's the enemy."

That deep, raspy voice sent chills down Cyan's spine. He sounded terrifying, as if he weren't a cyborg but more of a demon. His cold proclamation that she was the enemy didn't bode well for her. She had a bad feeling he had learned a lot from the brutal soldiers who had once had them under their thumbs.

The cyborg who walked into the room had long, free-flowing black hair to his waist. He wore all black leather and his skin was a pale, lustrous silvery shade. She looked at his face. Scars marred his cheek in two places and there were a few more along his jawline. She finally met his gaze. Shock tore through her while she stared into icy blue eyes. Her breath froze inside her lungs and her heart accelerated so fast it felt as if it would pound out of her rib cage.

She would have collapsed onto the floor if she hadn't been sitting. Her entire body quivered. The cyborg moved into the room enough for the door to close behind him.

"This is Krell," Onyx informed her. "Humans put those scars on him. I'd stop gawking at him if I were you. He gets angry when anyone does that. Krell, this is Cyan. At least that's what she said her name was when we captured her on Belta Station. She claims Earth Government sent her there to investigate the attack on it."

Cyan wasn't sure exactly how it happened but one second she sat and the next she stood. She couldn't take her gaze off Krell. *That is his name*, she thought, still in shock. *Krell*. It sounded so mean to her, harsh. She stumbled toward him. His generous mouth curved downward in a grimace and his face hardened into a dangerous expression at her approach but she moved slowly enough not to seem threatening. At least she hoped she didn't appear that way.

He stood at least six foot seven or so. Due to her five-foot-three height, he towered over her when she paused just inches from him. Her hand shook when it slowly rose. He held still, watched her with contempt and anger, but didn't strike out at her. She hesitated before her fingertips brushed the scarred side of his face. She couldn't miss the way his nose flared and the icy blue of his eyes seemed to darken more.

"Admiring the handiwork of your fellow soldiers?" His brutal, rough tone made her jerk. Pure rage emanated from him. He suddenly gripped her wrist but he didn't tear her hand away.

"Watch her," Onyx urged. "She's probably going for your eyes."

The grip on her wrist tightened painfully but he still didn't yank her hand away. She trembled hard as she continued to gently stroke his warm, scarred skin. Tears filled her eyes and her other hand opened to press against the leather at his stomach. He growled at her again, gripped that wrist too, but still didn't push her away. His frown deepened and it seemed that the level of his anger did too as he glared down at her.

Cyan opened her mouth to try to speak but she had to swallow first. She blinked back the tears just to see him clearly. The pain of his grip registered but it didn't matter. She licked her lips and nearly fell against him when her legs threatened to give out.

"You're really here. You made it. I thought for sure you'd died."

The cyborg glanced away from her to shoot an annoyed look toward Onyx. "Is she suffering from head trauma? This isn't the reaction I expected. Most humans would scream and cower from me."

"She's feisty and a trickster. Sky taught me those words. She's deceptively clever and tends to attack when you least expect it. Watch your nuts. She'll target them."

A growl rumbled from Krell as he glowered back at her from his impressive height. "Do it and I'll snap both your wrists."

"I remember you," she breathed. "You're alive." Tears slipped down her face. "I can't believe it. Did Mavo survive? Is he here somewhere? He

48

said you were his friend. I thought the guards had killed you when I saw your bloody body sprawled on that holding-cell floor before the escape."

His features paled and his eyes widened. Pain shot through her body when her ass connected with the floor. It took her seconds to realize he'd shoved her away from him. She looked up, had to push back strands of her long black hair to see him, and flinched over the pure rage in his icy glare, which was directed at her. Her heart wrenched at his hatred.

She shouldn't have approached him. She'd just been so stunned at seeing a familiar face. Chances were good if this male had survived then Mavo had as well. She cleared her throat, stayed on the floor, and assessed her injures. There'd be some bruises on her butt but he hadn't damaged her beyond that.

"Who are you?" Krell shook from fury. "What do you know about me or Mavo?"

"What is going on?" Onyx gasped. "What does this mean?"

"Who are you?" Krell advanced quickly, grabbed Cyan before she could react and viciously hauled her to her feet. Her back slammed into a wall and she found her body pinned by the enraged cyborg. One of his hands gripped her throat while his other arm hooked around her waist to hike her up his body until they were face level. He snarled at her. "How do you know that name?"

Her mouth opened but she cried out from the stabbing pain her brain suffered when she attempted to answer him. The hold on her throat eased but she felt his big body against hers. She reached up slowly to cup his face. She stared into his eyes, trying to convey that she wasn't the enemy.

49

"I'm a friend."

She tried to frantically work around the conditioning she'd endured for three years. Her father's team had really messed up her head, programmed her brain with the help of technology to keep her from saying too much. But as she stared at the cyborg inches from her face she hoped he'd be able to figure out what she couldn't say, as impossible as it seemed. She was grateful her father had never learned how close she'd been to her cyborg guard and he hadn't used Mavo's name as a pain trigger.

"Who are you?" he roared. "How do you know of Mavo?"

More tears slid down her face. "I've been conditioned. I can't tell you how I know him but I do. I'm his friend."

Confusion crossed Krell's features and some of his anger eased away before coldness swept his handsome face. "You somehow accessed computer records from our time on Earth. There had to be pictures of us with detailed information of our cyborg associations." He growled low inside his throat. "Stop messing with my mind. I will kill you. This isn't a path you want to take to spy for your government. We have no friends from Earth."

Heartache stabbed at her chest that he didn't believe she meant no harm. "It's not a trick. It's technology. I've been conditioned to never speak about it. I'll go into convulsions if I try." Her headache grew worse, she knew she bordered on blacking out and had to stop thinking and talking about the past.

"Answer me. Are you here to spy for Earth? Are they aware of our existence? Did they somehow extract information from Zorus that he wasn't aware of when they captured him? Are my people in danger? Is a military detail on its way to this section of space to hunt for us?" He snarled the words. "You're a soldier. Are you their scout? Did they order you to memorize files in case you found us, to make us trust you?"

She stared into his eyes and refused to answer. She couldn't. The headache started to dissipate, barely, and she breathed easier. The cyborg might be angry but at least she remained conscious.

"No," she whispered. "Please don't hurt me, Krell. I need to see Mavo."

He roared loudly, enough to make her ears ring. She gasped when he spun and her body was airborne. She hit the floor on her side, rolled into a wall, and lay there stunned.

"No!" Onyx yelled.

"She's a danger to our people and she just threatened Mavo." Krell snarled the words, pushed at the other cyborg and glared at her with murder glinting in his dark eyes.

Cyan lifted her head, ignored the pain the impact with the floor had sent throughout her body, and watched as Onyx tried to hold the bigger cyborg back to stop him from attacking her. Cyan knew, by the sheer magnitude of rage twisting his scarred features, that Krell would hurt her if he got his hands on her. She swept her gaze across the room.

She'd struck the chair when she'd been thrown. It had broken the metal leg off and she reached for the broken piece. It hurt to struggle to sit up but she rested her back against the wall. Krell shoved Onyx aside and snarled at her. She saw her impending torture in his chilling blue eyes. He noticed her weapon, his fists balled, and it became obvious he intended to finish her off.

She stared at him, hesitated from the dread of what would come, but still stabbed her thigh as hard as she could. The agony made her scream. She nearly blacked out from the intense, fiery pain and her hand released the metal. She writhed from how much it hurt to have the jagged, broken chair leg impaled in the top of her thigh.

Shock made both cyborgs freeze where they stood. Onyx recovered first. "Medic!" he yelled. "Get a medic!"

Cyan tore her gaze from the stunned Krell to stare at her thigh. Blood spread across the floor under her leg. The black material of her pants looked wet where the metal had breached and she had to fight tears from the intense pain. She peered up at Krell.

"Why did you do that?" Krell still gaped at her. "I wouldn't really have killed you."

The door opened and a cyborg rushed in carrying a white first-aid kit. He dropped to his knees, cursed, and tore open the box to access the medical equipment inside.

"This is your idea of getting answers?" The new cyborg sounded outraged. "You hit an artery."

A cold feeling numbed Cyan as she leaned back, refusing to look away from Krell. He watched her grimly. She knew the moment the medic gripped the metal and tore it free. She clenched her teeth, hissed out and knew the bleeding grew worse. She had a big hole in her leg.

"I didn't do it," Krell rasped. "She did. Very smart but this won't stop the interrogation, human. It will only delay it until you are treated."

Material tore as the medic ripped her pants open to expose the wound. He dumped liquid over her skin to clear the blood and stop the bleeding so he could inspect the wound. He gasped loudly.

She shifted her gaze when his head jerked up to stare at her. His darker gray, dusky skin turned a sickly shade of ashy, grayish white. She looked down but knew what she'd see—a ragged wound in her flesh and shiny metal where white bone should have been.

"This can't be," the medic whispered.

"What?" Onyx stepped closer.

The medic reached out to suddenly grab Cyan's face to pull her attention to him. "You look human. Your skin is flesh colored."

"She is human," Krell rasped.

Both Cyan and the medic turned to stare at Krell.

"No, she's not. At least not all the way. She's…" The medic's voice faded to silence.

Cyan watched Krell move closer, couldn't look away from him, and knew the moment he saw what the medic had. He jerked his shocked gaze to hers.

"You're a cyborg?"

"Not quite," she whispered, in too much pain to do more. "But close. I'm not a spy and I'd never hurt cyborgs."

Krell reeled backward until his back hit the wall. His blue eyes were wide, stunned, perhaps even a little horrified, and Cyan watched him. The medic seemed to recover, tending to the painful wound. He'd stopped the bleeding and Cyan tried hard to ignore how much it hurt as he began to cauterize some of the damage that would start bleeding again quickly once the liquid that froze the blood started to thaw.

Onyx cursed before he rushed outside the room. The long-haired cyborg with the icy-blue eyes kept her attention. He was her link to Mavo and the only familiar face she'd seen since running into cyborgs.

Chapter Three

"What is she?"

The cyborg council, at least ten of them, stood in the hallway outside Cyan's room where she sat handcuffed by one wrist to a med bed. They were visible through the open door and she could hear them.

The doctor hesitated. "I've never seen anything similar to her, to be honest. She's mostly organic but her bones are made of a metallic substance that isn't the same as our enhanced bones. Her rib cage is..." The doctor sighed. "It's not just bones. The interior is enclosed to totally protect her heart and lungs. I'd guess it's an alloy that is resistant to weapons. Her tissues appear completely human until you see how quickly she's healing. I took a sample to study but it appears totally normal. No human could have survived having their bones removed to be replaced with what she has in there. I can only assume they made the frame and had to grow tissue around it. It's miraculous technology."

"Does she have implants?"

"Yes," the doctor stated. "Four inside her brain but they were near impossible to detect through whatever material they used for her skull. When you scan it, it reads as if she has a totally human brain. It appeared too perfect though so I managed to wire in a tiny camera to go under the skull at the base of her neck. That's when I noticed the shadows of the devices. From where they are located I'd say two of them are linked to her speech and thought areas. I have no idea what the other two are for or what they might do. It's not a mapped part of the brain that I'm knowledgeable about. They aren't placed where I've ever seen them. On scans you'd swear she has human bones but she doesn't. When I closed her thigh I was able to get a good look at the metal. I didn't take a sample because it might have crippled her. The only way to do it is if I removed an inch of the material and I'm not even certain what would cut through it. I may have had to take the entire leg at a joint. I refuse to do that."

One of the council members turned his head toward her. "Has she talked?"

"She just states she's been conditioned not to give out information relevant to what she is or her purpose of creation. I'm assuming those implants connected to her brain are there to prevent her from sharing classified information such as her designation. They seem to trigger intense pain if she attempts it. She has tried to cooperate." The doctor glanced at her before looking back at the council. "She inflicted that injury to show us what she couldn't put into words. Otherwise we never would have known she wasn't what she appeared to be. Every test, every scan, comes back human. Even her blood work doesn't raise flags. Whoever created her had technology I've never seen before or thought possible."

A female cyborg council member wearing a red two-piece outfit moved away from the group to walk inside Cyan's room. She paused at the door and smiled warmly.

"My name is Jazel. I am one of twelve cyborg council members." Her pale-blonde hair was a striking contrast against her dull, deep-gray skin tone. "What is your name?"

56

"Cyan." She paused. "My official name is Cyan Eous."

The tall cyborg crept a little closer. "You've caused quite a stir in our community."

"I bet."

"Are you a cyborg?"

"No." Cyan paused again. "I don't know. I don't think so but we have similarities."

"Were you cloned?"

"No, I know I wasn't cloned, but I wasn't given many details." A headache stated to throb in the back of her head. "Talking about it causes pain. We're bordering on me screaming in agony. Can we change the subject?"

"We're very curious about you."

"I know."

"Did Earth Government send you to track us down?"

"No." The pain eased. "They sent me after Markus Models. They are a defense android line that didn't work out so well. An Earth company made them too smart and the creepy things think they are alive but they aren't."

"The same has been said of us."

"They are totally different from you. I'm aware of your kind. These things are not people. They are cold, killing machines that have decided they are alive but they don't have souls. They share mind links, don't even have their own personalities, and decided to kill anything breathing since they believe their so-called race is better than any other."

57

More council members and the doctor entered the room but they hung back, allowing Jazel to be their spokesperson. Cyan glanced at them but focused on the cyborg female.

"The government doesn't know about me." Cyan paused. "Only my father and his team knew I was no longer fully human."

"Who was your father?"

Pain throbbed. "I can't say. I'm supposed to say his name was Edward Pack, there's an entire history created for me to assure my past is covered, and every fifteen years it changes."

"Why?"

"I don't age." Cyan tried not to show the relief she experienced over being able to tell someone, anyone, something true about her life. "Every fifteen years I retire from Earth Government and take a few years off before I reenlist in another branch. They believe I'm my own daughter."

One of the council members moved forward. "I am called Coval. You expect us to believe this? They do intensive scans."

"I'm an excellent hacker." Cyan met his curious gaze. "And I have access to a lot of their hive information networks thanks to my father's connection to the government. They don't change passwords often and they are slow to add new technology. It's not difficult to upgrade the information they keep on me, switch out the files, or erase them. When I reenlist nothing is triggered."

"Why do you work for them if they don't know what you are?"

58

Cyan sighed, staring at Jazel. "What else am I going to do? I'm stronger than most humans, I have been trained to fight, and for the most part I don't draw any attention as a soldier."

"Are we your enemies?"

"No," Cyan stated sincerely. "Can I talk to…?" She was half afraid she'd set someone off in a rage once again. "Mavo? I knew him from before this was done to me."

The doctor inched closer. "She claims this was done to her while she was an adult. We couldn't get much else out of her without triggering the pain implants. She stated yes when I asked if she used to be human."

Jazel gasped, stunned, and gawked at Cyan. "You were once fully human?"

"Yes. My body suffered traumatic injury during your rebellion from Earth." Her head started to throb again and she reached up with her free wrist to rub her temple. "This was done to me to save my life."

The council members backed away and the doctor spoke. "She claims she helped us escape. I requested Mavo be sent here but it was denied. Onyx said Krell is convinced it's a trap."

It hurt that Mavo wouldn't arrive any time soon, if ever. Cyan tried to hide the tears that threatened to spill. "I need to see Mavo. I gave him the launching override codes to the shuttles. We were friends."

"That's impossible," a new male voice sputtered.

A tall black-haired cyborg entered the room. Cyan regarded him warily. He appeared angry, out of sorts, and glared at her. She hesitated.

59

"Mavo needs to talk to me if you want to figure this out. I did give him the codes. Tell him that and he'll know who I am. He can figure out what I can't say."

The new cyborg paled. "Impossible. That young human was Emily Pleva."

A sharp jab of pain shot through her brain but she managed not to scream. A few of the cyborgs reacted to the name, or what had once been her name. They knew of Edward Pleva. He had started the cyborg project, created them to be a disposable workforce for Earth Government, and he'd been feared by all.

"Yes," Cyan admitted carefully, trying to word things in a way that wouldn't set off her implants, waiting for the pain to strike. "You know how insanely smart he could be with creating living beings with his research." She carefully avoided saying the name Pleva. It would have sent her into convulsions instantly. "He couldn't stand to watch me die. I'd been ill for a while and he'd started a special secret project to find a way to extend my life. He and his team rushed me inside his lab after I was critically injured during the escape and I woke weeks later with this." She waved at her body. "Six inches shorter, totally not the same in appearance, yet here I am."

The dark-haired cyborg continued to glare at her. "I don't believe it. You somehow accessed the information and are trying to fool us."

"Zorus," the female cyborg warned softly, "listen to her."

Cyan sighed, wary of the headache. "I understand your suspicion. I really do. I don't even blame you but that's the truth. I used to be that girl you mentioned but now I have this body. I'm the same inside, for the most part, but they messed with my brain to protect me from revealing who I really am. The Government instantly ordered me to be executed as a traitor since I helped with the escape. My father wasn't about to lose me again. They conditioned my mind and used implants for anything those didn't cover until it's a landmine of triggers for certain words and information. Of course I never wanted to tell anyone the truth until now. I may not have had much of a life but it beat dying."

"If this is true, which I doubt," Zorus growled, "why didn't you seek us out beforehand?"

"Earth Government kept reporting that none of you had survived. I never heard any conflicting reports besides scary space stories that tended to be bullshit to keep humans from venturing out into pirate-controlled regions of deep space. You can bet I would have tried to find Mavo if I'd known he had survived."

"Zorus?" Jazel tried to get the dark-haired cyborg's attention. "Order Mavo to report for duty. We need him to talk with her to verify this story. We need confirmation if she is the human related to Doctor Pleva. He has information only she would know."

La la la, Cyan thought, trying to block out the conversation to keep her implants from inflicting pain. She remembered a trick Bella had taught her to use when hearing her father's name caused pain and tried it. *It's just a history lesson. Not personal. Not about me*. The pain eased and she relaxed, hoping hearing them discuss the past wouldn't hurt now.

"I won't do that to him. This is deception." Zorus glared at Cyan. "I won't subject him to your cruel game. He loved that human and her death

61

devastated him. He's never emotionally recovered. You may not have any compassion but I do. He thought of her as a friend and perhaps even as his child. It took him a long time to find peace from the guilt of leaving her behind."

It made Cyan's heart ache to think of Mavo suffering year after year. She could relate. She'd never stopped thinking about him. Every sleep cycle she'd imagined his face inside her mind to keep his memory alive. He'd been the only man she ever loved despite him not returning those feelings in the way she'd hoped.

"I don't want him to suffer." She stared at Zorus. "Don't make him come here to talk to me."

Coval cleared his throat. "We have a dilemma. She's not human and she may be more cyborg than she admits. What do we do with her?"

"Keep her locked up," Zorus ordered. "When she's cleared from Medical send her to detention. We can't have her running around. We aren't sure of what she truly is or what her actual motives are. For all we know, she could be a spy sent from Earth. I'd like to believe her but we can't risk the lives of our people."

"I protest," one of the male cyborg council members sputtered. "She's an attractive female and if she's a cyborg despite her coloring, we can't ignore that." He glanced at the doctor. "What is the condition of her reproductive system?"

"Healthy," the doctor announced. "She can breed."

Cyan's mouth dropped open. "Excuse me?"

Jazel sighed. "It's law on Garden, our planet, that every cyborg breeds at least one child to help the advancement of our race. Our females are fewer in numbers. You need to take at least two males into a family unit if you are a cyborg. You will be ordered to produce at least three children, one for each of you."

"No way in hell," Cyan hissed, shooting a glare at the guys in the room. "Anyone touches me and I'll slice your nuts off. I'm not a baby factory."

Jazel gave her a sympathetic look. "I understand but it's a necessity. You are probably a cyborg and a part of our community. You need to follow our laws."

Rage burned in Cyan. "This is what you've allowed your society to become?" She fixed her anger on Zorus since he seemed to be in charge. "Earth Government told you what and when to eat. How to live. Even who you had to have sex with. You wanted freedom and real lives," she raged. "You fought for the right to make your own choices. Earth used to be the enemy. When did you decide to use their playbook to force people to be breeders?"

Zorus paled.

"You escaped, risked everything, and you're telling me you make others go through that same bullshit now? You order them how to live and even how many kids they must have? Even Earth banned those breeding tests."

The cyborg leaned forward, still pale, and stared at her. "You're really angry."

"You bet I am." She wanted to lunge at him and do damage. "I…" She paused, her headache grew worse, remembering the past. She had to avoid personal detail. Anything she discussed with the cyborgs had to be nonspecific to her former life, her actions. She took a few calming breaths. *History lesson—use that trick*, she ordered her mind. It helped ease the pain as she carefully reworded what she wanted to say, trying to pull her memory away from vivid details, focusing on her anger instead.

"A human betrayed everyone who trusted her to do the ethical thing. It seems she cared more about granting you rights than you did if this is what you've done to the society you built. What is wrong with you?" She shot venomous looks at every cyborg in the room. "They used to tell people that you couldn't think for yourselves, that you needed them to do it for you, and maybe they were right."

"We don't need humans," Coval grunted.

Thinking so much about the past caused severe pain and she grabbed the back of her head but kept glaring at them. "Someone didn't suffer all that, risk her ass, and lose the life she had just so you could do this to your own people. Shame on you."

Zorus reeled back. "We didn't want it this way. There were so few females. We needed to increase our numbers."

"Yeah, and your creator said he needed to do research when he tortured your kind," she spat, directing her anger at him. "Earth Government wanted people they could send on suicide missions that nobody would care or protest about when they died. That's why they funded your creation. They deemed you expendable. You're just like the man who made you." She swept her angry gaze over each of them. "You're more human than you thought. You've become the thing you hated most. Congratulations."

Zorus shook his head in denial. "We don't, I didn't—"

Cyan cut him off, so angry she forgot to be careful of what she said. "Didn't you? Do you know how terrified I was when I sneaked information to you? What I risked to save you?" She glared around the room. "I'm the reason you got away. I hacked my father's computer to get the override codes to those shuttles you used to blast away from the surface. I hacked into those ships you stole in orbit to prevent them from opening fire on you the second you entered space and allowed you to board them so easily. I took a bullet to my chest because I refused to stop someone from getting control of the tarmac cannons to fire at you while you fled. I put those shuttles on the ground by screwing with the supply orders to make sure there were plenty available at the time of your escape. They busted into my office, demanding I unhook from the system, but I refused. I lasted long enough to send the system into reboot to give you those minutes to make it into space while I lay dying on a floor. I believed you were real people with the ability to have normal lives. To love who you wanted to be with, have that choice, and you're telling me you shit all over the very reasons you wanted freedom so bad? Get out. I think I'm going to be sick." The pain was so bad she knew she had only moments until unconsciousness or seizures overtook her. She had to regain control, steady her breathing and focus. *Think before you speak!*

Zorus paused by the door. "Clear the room." He still appeared pale. Jazel hesitated. "Get out," Zorus snarled. "All of you."

The room emptied until only Cyan and Zorus remained. They watched each other. Cyan wished she could hobble out of bed and slap the jerk. He seemed shaken.

"We had to ensure our future survival. We are nothing similar to Earth Government."

"Yeah, that's the same bullshit your creator said when he explained how he could create a race of people to be abused and sent on death missions. He said it was to ensure the survival of humans." Her chest ached from the sadness that overwhelmed her and made her pain seem tame in comparison. "You've made it a law to force women to be breeders? What is wrong with you? What is so different about you than them? You think about that long and hard. There's always a good reason for the shitty things people do. It still doesn't make it right, does it?"

"Are you really E—"

"Don't!" she yelled, cutting him off before the agonizing pain hit. "Don't say that name. It hurts me."

He inched closer, his features softening as he examined her. He didn't attempt to repeat the name she'd been born with.

"That girl dreamed about what kind of future she could give the cyborgs she loved so much by freeing all of them. It was the one meaningful thing she could do with her short life." She paused, refusing to cry. "Get out. I meant what I said about how you should be ashamed."

"It became about priorities."

66

"It should have been about happiness and giving your people the rights they fought and died for when they rebelled. I swore I'd never kill a cyborg and I won't. I promise you though if some asshole tries to turn me into a breeder I will castrate him. I won't become a baby machine. A woman fought for your kind once and she'd do it again."

He watched her silently. "We've realized recently that we made mistakes."

Her shoulders sagged. "Please just leave. I'm having a bad day. I discovered you survived, made total crap out of the freedom you've been given, and now once again the body I've been put into has another drawback. You wouldn't try to force your laws on me if I were totally human. I don't want anything to do with you if this is what you've become."

"Our creator was brilliant if not mentally damaged in his logic."

"Yeah."

"He is deceased?"

"He passed eleven years ago. He planned to do this." She patted her good leg. "Take on a newer, younger body, but he didn't get the chance. He died too suddenly to reach his lab. He wanted to wait as long as possible to avoid losing his prestige but he also feared if the Government knew it was possible to trade out bodies they'd realize what he'd done for me. He had to choose to remain who he was or become someone new. He may have been a monster but he didn't totally suck."

"I'll consider telling Mavo about you. A familiar face may comfort you, E—" He barely avoided saying her name.

"That name actually causes me intense pain. I'm Cyan now." She met his stare. "I don't want to hold on to anything from that life anymore. The one good thing she ever did has turned out to be a sad, horrible thing."

His mouth opened but she held up her hand to silence him.

"Don't. You can't excuse what you've done. Don't tell Mavo I'm here. I don't want to cause him any more pain and I'm so angry that I'd say things that will shred him if he's half the man he used to be. I shouldn't have ever told any of you anything but seeing that tall, scarred cyborg made me stop protecting myself because I knew who he was. I hoped something from my past remained—a friend—but I don't have any. Not here, not with your kind, and I just want to be alone. Lock me up and throw away the key. Just don't think I'll allow you to force me to make more cyborgs. It won't happen."

Zorus hesitated. "No male will force you. I'll make sure of that."

Cyan watched Zorus turn and leave her room. Her eyes closed and she sank back against the pillows of the bed. She fought the urge to curl up onto her side and have a good cry. The "history lesson" had left her with a migraine. At least Mavo had survived, they'd been friends, and she'd loved him. That had to be enough to make up for the horrors she'd uncovered. He might live in a screwed-up society but he had escaped from Earth.

* * * * *

Anger burned through Krell as he glared at Zorus, who had buzzed at his front door to request admittance. He stood in the open doorway to block the man from entering him home. "What do you want?"

"I came from Medical."

"I don't want to discuss that treacherous spy. I didn't harm her leg. I admit I lost my temper when she mentioned Mavo's name but she touched me first. It was unnerving and I couldn't gauge her honesty for some reason until I realized she's not human. I was careful not to cause real harm with my rough treatment of her. I judged her weight and height, and adjusted the force I used so I wouldn't break any of her bones when I threw her. I made sure she'd land without severe damage. I only wanted to shake her up."

"I'm not here about that."

"What are you doing here? You're off duty. You promised your female, Charlie, no business during your honeymoon."

"Charlie understood when I explained after the council informed me of the female's unknown origins. I wanted to see and speak to her myself. I did that and now I'm here."

"Why? You have no reason to chew me out for the harsh treatment of the prisoner."

"I need a favor."

"No." Krell tried to close the door.

Zorus struck his hand out, halting it. "I believe her."

Shock rolled through Krell. "You're growing soft and foolish. I am glad I've never experienced love if this is what it does. She's a spy from Earth."

"She raged at me after Jazel informed her she needed to conform to our laws. She said enough to make me believe she is Emily Pleva, Krell. Her father was a brilliant scientist. He somehow managed to give her a new body."

"Impossible. Mavo talked nonstop about his precious human for years after we escaped. She was dying of an incurable disease that slowly ceased the functions of her body. I saw her from a distance a few times while on Earth. She was heavyset and I could tell she was tall despite her being dependent upon a device that moved her body while sitting. Also, she had to be hooked to machines. She had totally different coloring, the face isn't the same, and she'd never have survived this long. She also wouldn't appear so youthful, regardless of what Earth scientists can do to slow the aging process."

"Edward Pleva created us. Why couldn't he create a body for someone he loved when it would have been the most significant project of his career? She was his only child. I am aware of facts that you weren't. I was part of the group who planned our escape and know how much his daughter did to help us. She's the reason we are free now. If that is her, which I believe, we owe her."

"I don't."

Zorus cocked his head. "Did Mavo ever tell you how he knew you'd been taken from the group before we rebelled or how he arrived to carry you out of that holding cell? Did you ever consider it lucky that the fire alarms began while the human guards were torturing you to death? I'm also friends with Mavo. He was with her when the alert on her system notified her that a cyborg had been taken to detention. She sent him after you and lured the guards away." He paused. "Not only did she save your life but she gave you freedom as well."

Krell took a deep breath. "Understood, but I don't believe she's really that human."

"You're the best interrogator we've ever had. That's why I've come here. You owe Emily Pleva your life. There's also the fact that you're friends with Mavo."

"What do you want?" Krell had a feeling he'd hate the answer.

"I don't want to lock her up in a detention cell. We owe her more than that. I have not grown soft, Krell. I'm being logical. It's possible that Edward Pleva could have somehow put his daughter into a new body. He did love her and we concluded she was his only weakness. You would have been convinced as I am that it's possible if you'd heard her rage at the council and me over our breeding laws. I actually experienced shame." He gave a small smile. "She made good points."

"Earth Government must have figured exactly how we were able to escape and are using that information to plant her with us to spy. That is logical as well." He paused, his mind working. "How would she know about our breeding laws? That's proof of her treachery. When you were taken back to Earth they must have extracted information from you that you aren't aware of."

"I didn't break. Coval made the point that she's female, not human, and shouldn't be detained in a holding cell. The council was visiting her and held the discussion in her room. Jazel explained our breeding laws to her and how she needed to join a family unit with two males. She's physically

71

able to breed. Since she's alone, new, they expect her to be handed into one as soon as they decide who to give her to. She compared us to Earth Government."

An uneasy feeling settled into the pit of Krell's stomach. "You're going to force her to join with males she doesn't know and not give her a choice of which ones will be a part of her family unit? That's harsh. She's not human but she's possibly some form of upgraded version of us. We wouldn't do that to one of our own."

Zorus watched him silently. "Perhaps. She's been deemed healthy for reproduction. While she's smaller than our female cyborgs, it won't harm her. She has threatened to castrate any male who attempts it."

"What do you want?" Krell released the doorjamb and crossed his arms over his chest.

"I want to send her here. I will tell the council you'll be perfect for her. I'm certain you will learn how to read her enough to discover if she's telling the truth or if she's lying. It's what you do best. You will get to the bottom of this mystery."

"No."

"What if she is Emily Pleva? Do you want to tell Mavo you could have protected her from another male who may agree with the majority of the council that assigning her into a family unit is the only option? Do you think he'll be thrilled if that male decides to force the issue? She's attractive, on Garden with strangers, and vulnerable."

Krell clenched his teeth. "That's low. No male would harm her."

"Are you certain? Some of us hold grudges against humans and she appears to be a human. They may not give her the respect due a cyborg female. Some may even logically assume she isn't to be given the option of saying no to physical contact. What are the odds of a male not touching her when she's been given to him? If he has a good friend or has friends who have been waiting for a female to join with them, who is to say he won't accept them into the family unit? It will be up to the primary male to make those decisions in her case. He'll have total control of what happens to her since she won't be given rights to make her own choices."

"You're talking about a male inside a family unit. You said you wanted me to guard her." Alarms were triggered inside Krell's brain.

"The council was waiting to speak to me after I left her room. They want her joined into a family unit immediately. I couldn't talk them out of it and the majority overruled my objections. They refuse to send her to detention but she can't be trusted either. The logical choice was assigning her to a family unit with at least one male to care for her and to help her adjust to life on Garden. They are planning on convening in the morning to go over candidates to find the appropriate male to give her to."

He shook his head. "No." He backed up, his hands lowered to his sides, and he glared at Councilman Zorus. "I am not a male to ever join into a family unit. I am not obligated to do so."

"You're scarred and damaged but still eligible if you wish to join one. That was your choice to option out and the council agreed, considering your odds of finding a female willing to take you on were very low."

73

"I'm undesirable. Our women don't want me because of my damaged appearance."

"You won't force her into a physical relationship and you are antisocial." Zorus stepped inside his home, closed the door and lowered his voice. "You intimidate and frighten other cyborg males. None will be eager to try to persuade you into sharing her inside a family unit. I know you won't hurt her."

"No." There was no way he wanted a female, especially that one, and Zorus couldn't make him agree.

"What if she really is Emily Pleva? She saved all of our lives and Mavo will eventually hear about her. I'll have to tell him that I came to you, explained the situation, and you didn't even try to protect her. He's still your friend, isn't he? I heard he named one of his sons after you and listed that child as your required replacement. He had a child and registered it as yours, just to alleviate your duty to produce one. I can use public opinion to give her an exemption from our laws if you're able to determine she really is the human who helped us rebel. Every cyborg knows Emily Pleva was the one human who has always been our friend. They'll see her as such and not as a cyborg. Our laws won't apply to her. She won't be forced to live with males she doesn't wish to. She's very set against it. Think of how much that would mean to Mavo if you protected her. He's done a lot for you."

"We should contact Mavo, have him return to Garden and speak with the prisoner. He could determine if she's telling the truth. He knew her well."

"But what if she is a spy and not his precious human? Do you remember how torn he was? The agony and guilt he suffered leaving her behind after all she'd done for us? He felt certain she suffered punishment for her actions. It would rip open those old wounds that have healed if he's given hope she is who she claims to be but tear him apart if she's not. I would really prefer he not find out about this until we're certain of who we are truly dealing with. I can prevent him from learning about this while he's assigned on the *Vontage* with Steel. I can even extend their mission to give you a few weeks to discover the truth. That way when the ship returns home we'll be able to tell him the truth."

"You're an asshole."

A grin suddenly curved the other cyborg's mouth. "So are you. We both care about Mavo and he cares about that human. We don't want him to be hurt."

Krell knew when he'd been outmaneuvered. That would be the sinking feeling inside his gut and the anger that heated his blood. "There will be no joining ceremony. This isn't real. It's temporary. I'll prove she's a spy, unworthy to live, or that she is Emily Pleva. This nonsense ends as soon as I am certain either way."

"Agreed." Zorus had the nerve to chuckle. "I'll inform the council that you wish to join with her. They'll easily agree since she acknowledged she knew you from before or at least claimed to. It will be a relief to them to avoid making that decision."

"I never met her while on Earth."

75

"They'll be happy to have a resolution. You're a good candidate." Zorus paused. "Is your sperm viable? That may be considered by them as a negative if it isn't."

"I'm not touching her."

"I know that but the council doesn't."

"Unbelievable," Krell growled. "I have viable sperm if I take the injections to activate it. I am not completely sterile."

"Perfect. I see nothing for the council to object to."

"She won't agree." Hope soared inside Krell at that prospect. He'd thrown the female across a room and while she hadn't been afraid of his appearance, she wouldn't welcome it. "You said it yourself. She is very set against joining a family unit."

Zorus smiled. "I'll handle that. Make an appointment with Medical to get the shots. We want this to look good. I have a friend there who owes me a favor. I'll contact him, make him agree to state that you took the shots, and after he agrees, I'll tell you who to see." Zorus hesitated. "You refused to put name markings on your body due to your abundance of scars. I'll tell the council you still hold an aversion to putting more on your body to explain your lack of wishing a joining ceremony to be performed. They'll accept that easily."

"I'm not touching her."

"You won't have to and you don't really have to take the shots to activate your sperm but we want all the paperwork to appear real. That's why I'm calling in the favor." Zorus spun, opened the door and sailed out.

Krell glared at the closed door and growled. "I hate that jerk."

Chapter Four

Cyan watched the big cyborg cautiously as Krell's cold blue gaze raked down her body. His scars were revealed clearly, his long black hair pulled back inside a leather thong behind his neck in a long braid that fell to his waist, and she was pretty certain he'd purposely done it to intimidate her. He wasn't wearing a uniform now. Instead he wore a black tank top that showed off the scars on his throat and his arms. More scars were displayed on his chest where the material didn't cover.

"I have a guestroom," he grunted, his raspy voice harsh. "You are not permitted to leave my home. I've been warned of your hacking skills if you are the human you claim to be. I will refrain from saying that name due to being told it causes you pain. The systems have been taken offline and only work manually with my palm print." He raised one hand, showed it to her, and his eyes narrowed. "You'd have to drag my unconscious body to the door lock to get it open. It would register if I didn't have a pulse." The hand tightened into a fist as it lowered to his side. "I wouldn't recommend attacking me. You'd lose."

"Okay." She took a deep breath. "My, aren't you friendly."

"Is that a joke?" He didn't appear amused.

"I guess not."

He growled under his breath. "This was not my idea and I'm not pleased with having a houseguest. I don't trust you. I believe you're still working for Earth Government but the council refused to detain you. You need around-the-clock supervision."

"And it was your lucky day?"

His blue eyes narrowed more.

"Keep doing that and you won't be able to see me." She mimicked him, hoping to draw a smile, and wondered how well he could see her. "You're blurry." She stopped squinting at him and smiled. "Who did you piss off to get this assignment?"

He frowned but his eyes opened fully. "It was determined by Councilman Zorus that you should stay here. He knows I won't touch you while other males might be inclined to do so."

"Touch me? As in 'I look human and they wanted to mess with my face because I'm the enemy' or in a way that would make me castrate them?"

"Either way. I don't beat on females without cause and I'm not interested in you physically."

"Good thing." Her gaze raked up and down him with a quick sweep. "You're huge. I can't say her real name either without it causing pain, so I'll call her Bee. She used to tell me that while she'd had a hand in creating males, she made everything size proportionate to their bodies. She had a twisted sense of humor and couldn't resist arguing that point in the developmental stages. She won that fight."

The cyborg frowned.

"Bee was your creator's assistant from the beginning. She helped him with every step of the process in creating cyborgs. She also fought to give you the ability to grow hair quicker because she had a thing for long-haired

78

men." Cyan shrugged. "She also hated hairy men from the neck down." She glanced at his black pants and her smile widened before she jerked it up to his face. "No manscaping needed."

"What does that mean?"

"It means you don't have a lot of body hair and you don't need to shave. You can thank a man on the team for having armpit hair. He said you'd look odd without it. Some Models were given a little chest hair because of him as well." She glanced at the bare skin showing above the material of his shirt, no hair in sight, and met his gaze again. "You didn't get any. You weren't designed for a mining assignment. They worked with their shirts off because of the extreme heat. He wanted those Models to fit in with human workers."

He stared at her for a long moment while Cyan shifted her stance. "Too personal? Sorry. I tend to babble when I'm nervous."

"What else do you know about us?"

She hesitated. "You were designed to be a security model. Your height and tankish body give it away. They wanted you to tower above the average human and be built for intimidation. Mission accomplished. You sure do that. I bet it's tough to find shirts big enough to fit you."

He said nothing.

"Be happy you aren't purple. That was Bee's favorite color but the guys on the team refused. They chose gray tones instead since they were ordered to make it obvious you weren't human. She wanted to go with a nice magenta, which is kind of bright and a little pink. It totally would have ruined the badass look you have going on."

Anger glinted in his eyes. "You find this amusing?"

"Not really but it beats us having a staring contest, doesn't it? You're not real talkative and that leaves it up to me to open a line of communication." She watched him.

"I'll take you to your room. I'm sure you're in need of rest."

"No. Please? I've been locked to a med bed and was about to go out of my mind. I'm used to activity. I'm not into sitting still much or a big sleeper."

He didn't speak and it started to bug her. She'd rather argue with him than just stand there mute. Anything would be better than being locked inside a room until she screamed from boredom. She studied his clothes, the way his muscles were tense, and glanced around the room. A workout area had been set aside and he had a punching bag, weights to lift and a lot of padded floor.

"Were you working out when I arrived?"

"Yes. I do that to stay fit and healthy."

"You were designed that way so it doesn't matter if you work out or not. You'll always look like this."

He growled at her in response.

She frowned. "Look, I'm the same way. I could eat and eat but I don't gain weight. It kind of sucks. I never thought I'd bitch about that but after a few decades you just want to change something, anything, but it doesn't happen. My body maintains and so does yours." She glanced down at her chest. "Be happy you're a defense model. I think they stole a sex bot design to make this body and scaled everything back but the breasts." She tilted

80

her head slightly, staring at him. "Talk about uncomfortable. I wonder how long they had the body displayed inside the lab, in storage. They don't clothe them, you know. The team who designed it had to have seen it every day. Yuck. Talk about needing therapy."

Emotion finally showed on his face when he expressed shock. "A sex bot?"

"Yeah. I've got double-D cups. Those are sex bot specifications. No other work Models or clones were made with breasts that size. I wish they hadn't screwed with my height though. I'm betting they did it to hide the fact that no Models were designed this small and it helped hide the fact that this body isn't totally human. I looked up the measurements for the sex bots and standard on them is about five foot seven or eight. They shortchanged me. That's a joke." She smiled. "Get it? Short and they changed me?"

He stared at her.

"Do you have a sense of humor at all? I'm trying real hard here to get you to crack a smile."

"No."

"Big surprise. Great. I'm locked up with the grim cyborg. Maybe you should call Councilman Zorus and tell him to assign me to someone else. At least jerks who want to beat on me or nail me would talk. You know, telling me I suck for being human-looking or how I should suck on them."

His mouth twitched.

"Ah ha! You almost smiled, didn't you?"

"No. That was a grimace. I understood the crude reference."

81

"I'm just grateful you got the innuendo. There's hope for you yet." She glanced at his workout area again. "Want to spar?" Her gaze slid to his. "Since you aren't much of a talker? I could use the physical outlet."

"It wouldn't be fair and your leg is injured."

She bent and removed her boots since he wasn't wearing any footwear. She removed her socks before she straightened. "I heal fast and the leg is all good now. I know it won't be fair but I'll try to go easy on you. I won't hurt you."

His mouth dropped open and his eyes widened before he hid his shocked response. "I meant it wouldn't be fair to you. You are no match for me."

She inched closer and grinned. "The bigger they are, the harder they fall. That's an Earth saying if you don't remember or never heard it. You're going down."

"You're serious? You want to spar with me?" He backed up into the center of the padded mats and actually smiled.

Cyan had to remember to breathe. It changed his face so much and despite the scars, she could tell he'd once been truly handsome. He still was—the scars on his face gave him a rakish, dangerous look. She followed him onto his training mats. Her hands rose, palms open, and she rolled her shoulders to loosen up.

"How about a little wager? If I win, you have to try to talk to me more, Krell. The tall, dark and moody thing drives me kind of nuts. I've spent too much time with an annoying computer over the past few weeks. Your doctors just wanted to ask me questions that gave me a migraine and that kind of ruined hearing another voice. Deal?"

"You're a soldier, correct? Earth Government trained you to fight?"

"Yes."

"I'm going to win. Their training wasn't sufficient."

"Really? What do you want from me if you win? Notice I said 'if'. Don't get too cocky."

"Silence for five hours."

"Ouch."

His hands lifted and his palms opened. She had to admit feeling a little relief at the gesture. She didn't want to box with the cyborg. A punch from one felt like hitting a wall, from what she remembered. He couldn't break her bones but he could cause damage to her body. Bruises or split skin hurt.

"Deal?" He almost appeared happy to her.

"Fine. Now I know you're going to kiss the mat, Too Tall. I can't shut up for that long."

"I'll take it easy on you. It will be considered my win after you're pinned flat and unable to move."

Cyan laughed. "You're so confident. I'll have to tell you all about my likes and dislikes after I pin you down. I like that in a man though. That bit of info was free."

He crouched a little, his blue eyes glinted with amusement, and it brought him down more to her level. It was a mistake but she appreciated him trying to even their heights out as much as possible. It told her he was into fair fights and it made her like him more.

"You come at me," he rasped in that deep, husky tone of his, "when you're ready to rest on the floor."

"You ready? I don't want you whining afterward that I took you by surprise."

He actually chuckled, a wonderful sound. "I'm prepared to enjoy five hours of non-chatter."

"I'll remember you said that and we'll talk about it." She suddenly lunged to his left and made him twist his upper body to try to follow her. She threw out an arm, nailing him in the hip.

He stumbled off balance, his crouched position already putting him at a disadvantage, and she pounced. Her fingers gripped his forearm, hot skin registered as she touched him, and she yanked him forward to put him totally off balance but used the hold to propel her at him in the same motion.

Their bodies collided but she had the advantage as they fell. She landed on top of him. He twisted onto his back a split second before he hit the mat and shock widened his eyes when he found her sprawled over his chest. She moved fast, threw a thigh over his hip, straddled him, and used her free hand to slam the palm of it into his diaphragm as she lifted to sit on his hips.

It knocked the air from his lungs as he hissed out a breath and her hold on his arm slid up to his shoulder. She used all the strength in her arm to pull as she lifted up, grabbed his hip and rolled him while he fought to catch his breath. Her weight collapsed onto his ass when she straddled him again, grabbed for his wrists and yanked them behind his back, twisting them up to the point she knew he'd feel pain but it wouldn't hurt him too much.

"What is that I hear, Krell? Did you say uncle?"

He gasped in air and his body tensed under hers. She clamped her knees on his hips tightly, lifted her feet, hooked them between his partially spread thighs and leaned forward enough to jerk them apart. Muscles strained and she knew she was going to hurt later from pulling a few but she managed to spread his thighs enough to make it harder for him to roll back over.

He snarled, not really a word but it might have been a curse. His head reared back but she jerked hers to the side just in time to avoid him smashing her face with the back of his skull. He tried to roll but with his arms twisted up his back and held in the center of his spine, he couldn't find any leverage.

"You're pinned, Too Tall."

When his body felt as if it turned to stone under her she actually experienced fear. He was stronger and in a lengthy fight, he'd win. She'd had surprise to her advantage and knew she couldn't hold him down for long.

He took some deep breaths but only turned his head to stare at her over his shoulder. Anger burned in those chilly blue eyes. "I could get free but I'd have to seriously injure you."

"Don't be a sore loser."

She released his wrists and her legs relaxed. She managed to bite back a groan as pain shot up her thigh to her butt. That move would cost her for sure but she'd heal within a few hours from the muscle damage. The guy was really strong. She didn't move from her seat on his ass but she did straighten.

He suddenly rolled and surprised her. Cyan gasped as her back hit the mat and she ended up pinned under about two hundred sixty pounds of muscular cyborg. He moved fast, jerked her arms above her head to secure her wrists with his hands, and since she'd been sitting on him with her legs spread, his hips ended up snugly cradled between her thighs. She swallowed and stared up at him with a little worry. He wasn't crushing her but enough of his weight rested on top of her that she could barely draw breath.

"How did you do that?"

She stared into his eyes. "You underestimated me. It's a common mistake. I am short, appear to be totally human, but I'm stronger than they are. Faster."

His gaze lowered to her mouth and he adjusted his weight to ease some of it off her chest. It did however move his hips as he slid a few inches upward. Her eyes widened and her lips parted in surprise. That wasn't just his hips pressed against her. Something hard and thick wedged along the seam of her pants.

"Are you angry?"

He met her gaze again. "I'm surprised and slightly irritated but the latter is directed at myself."

"I guess it's okay to point out that I pinned you first and that means I won."

The chill returned to his eyes. "That would be a fair assessment. What do you want to talk about?"

She hesitated. "Do you always get a hard-on when you fight or should I feel worried that we're really about to do this for real? I'm not having sex with you."

He suddenly lifted off her, stood, but bent over to offer her a hand up. She hesitated but placed hers inside his. He pulled her to her feet fast enough to give her a head rush and she stumbled. His other hand shot out to grip her hip to steady her. His long fingers curved there and remained. They studied each other.

"I apologize." His cheeks appeared to darken slightly on his pale, silvery skin. "It was the adrenaline rush."

"Uh-huh." She took a step back and he released her. "Okay. I'll buy that." *Don't look*. Her gaze still shot downward despite her mental order. The outline of his engorged cock was clear through his pants. "Shit. Size proportioned is right." Her gaze jerked up to his face and she realized she'd actually said that aloud. "Sorry! Maybe we shouldn't talk. Where is this room you said I could sleep in?"

He backed away and turned his body to try to hide the fact that the material of his pants was thin and he obviously wasn't wearing underwear since his cock strained against the front of them. "It's down the hall, first door to the left."

She spun, frantically looked for an escape, and caught a glimpse of the hallway. She didn't bother retrieving her boots or socks. Her heart hammered as she quickened her pace to put space between them.

The room was average sized, very sparse on furnishings, and besides the bed it only contained a nightstand. No entertainment unit adorned the wall. She closed the door and leaned against it.

The guy was hung. She doubted she'd ever get the image out of her head of the grim cyborg sporting wood. *More like a mast*, she amended, and shook her head in disgust at her sense of humor. *Up note, he's not as robotic as he seems*. She grinned. *And tough women turn him on.*

Krell turned and punched the bag when he heard Cyan's door close. He glared down at his wayward cock and clenched his teeth. He hadn't had sex with a woman in years. Cyborg females found him boring, unattractive or emotionally undesirable. He rarely left Garden despite Mavo asking him to go on a few off-world assignments on some of the ships they'd acquired. He'd mentioned sex bots and a space station where the artificial females wouldn't notice the scars or be intimidated by his size.

Krell had felt insulted at the time when his friend had made that suggestion. He'd be better off seeing to his own needs than playing with an animated sex doll. Cyan's body flashed in his mind. She was too short, too small, but perfect otherwise. She believed she'd been modeled after a sex bot. He might have been too hasty to assume one wouldn't be appealing.

He stared down at his cock again, grateful that it had softened since she'd fled the room, and closed his eyes. He accessed his implants and reconfigured his physical responses, shutting down the connection between his thoughts and his dick. Next time he wouldn't get an erection in front of the spy.

Her heaving breasts, which had nearly spilled from the top of her shirt, wouldn't get a response from his body in that manner again. He might notice their soft swell, imagine what it would be like to tear open her shirt to touch them, but he wouldn't embarrass himself by allowing her to know the direction his thoughts had traveled.

A bell chimed and he opened his eyes, spun and walked to the wall. He touched the pad to open mental communications as he lowered his mental shielding to allow his projected thoughts to be picked up. "What?"

"Has she arrived?"

"Yes. She's inside the guestroom."

"You need to get to know her, learn how to read her correctly and discover if she's telling the truth. You can't do that if she's in another room."

"Don't tell me how to do my job, Zorus. Where is Charlie? Isn't your female demanding your attention?"

"She's taking a shower while I prepare our food. I just wanted to check in with you."

"Stop bothering me. You already forced me to deal with this female. Isn't that enough for you?"

Zorus laughed, sure to amplify the sound in the connection, and Krell grunted in response, sending that clearly too.

"Talk to her. Watch her features and do what you do best. You will learn how to detect her lies. I heard you showed up at Medical. The paperwork was received at the council building. They believe you activated your sperm. Thank you."

"You're lucky I didn't have to actually take the shots. I'd have borrowed an extra one to jam into your nuts just for the pleasure of it."

Zorus laughed again. "I see having company doesn't improve your disposition. I almost feel sorry for that female. The faster you can prove who she is, the faster you can get her out of your home."

"Save your pity for your own female. It amazes me that she doesn't kill you while you sleep. End transmission." He jerked his hand away from the pad, cut the link with his mind as well, and spun. "Bastard."

He stormed through his home to the guestroom. Zorus had made a good point. The faster he learned how to read the female, the quicker she'd be sent away. It didn't matter to him if that would be to a detention center for being their enemy or if they gave her a home of her own. He just wanted her out of his. He knocked.

Get to know her, learn her facial expressions, her weaknesses, and pay attention to her pulse rate. Read her and get her out of my home. He blew out air. *Quickly.*

Chapter Five

Cyan opened the door carefully, wondering if he'd forgotten to give her some new order. He'd already told her not to leave his home. Krell towered in the hallway, his head nearly touched the ceiling, and a frown firmly curved his lips.

"You won the bet and I'll talk to you."

Don't look down at his crotch. It's tempting, but don't. She managed to keep her gaze from dropping and took a deep breath. He was trying to make an effort and she was bored.

"All right. That would be great. I have a million questions."

He backed up, giving her room to follow him into the living area. That statement earned her a suspicious glare before he spun around to stalk away, leaving her to trail behind, admiring his firm ass. He dropped into a big black chair, pointed to one opposite him, and she remembered he was supposed to be good at interrogating prisoners. She bet that was his real reason for wanting to have a conversation.

She sat, crossed her arms under her breasts, and the staring contest began. She lost, blinked first, and it annoyed her enough to speak. "What do you do for fun on this planet besides work out?"

"I analyze data and evaluate threat assessments to my people."

She swallowed. "Okay. And that's fun?"

"I enjoy working and I don't have to spend time with others except for designated meetings to update the other analysts and compare our information."

"You work from home?"

"Yes."

Silence stretched. "Do you date? Have friends? Have some kind of weird ritual you do?"

That drew a frown. "Weird ritual?"

"Perhaps go jogging in the morning?"

"You consider jogging a weird ritual?"

"Yes. Unless something is running from me that I have to catch or something scary is chasing me, I don't run. It's just weird to think it's fun otherwise."

His mouth twitched again.

"Another grimace or did you nearly smile?"

"What do you do on Earth for fun?"

"I don't spend a lot of time there. I'm usually assigned to one of the orbiting ships. In my off-duty hours I try to avoid men. Otherwise I guess my fun consists of hurting them."

"Why?"

"There aren't many females who enjoy being assigned off the surface and the males outnumber women seventeen to one on ships. They do dumb things often."

"I don't understand."

"They either think I'm a source of amusement by putting me down for being a woman or think I'm onboard for them to sexually harass. I don't take kindly to either endeavor. It's kind of fun to toss them onto their asses. Sometimes I play holoball with the computer. It doesn't slam into me on purpose to cop a feel."

"To what?"

She bit her lip. "Maul me. You know, bump into me to grope my ass or my breasts."

He frowned. "Humans are crude. Are you joined in a family unit?"

"No way." She shook her head.

"You are antisocial?"

"Let's just say I've dated over the years but it never worked out. I learned to just avoid the entire uncomfortable situation."

His icy blue eyes narrowed. "What was uncomfortable about dating?"

He was talking. It might not be about something she wished to discuss but it beat the silence. "Well, first off I always knew it couldn't be anything long-term. I don't age. I think after a decade or so they'd start to notice. There was also the whole faking-my-death thing I have to do after a certain amount of time. I didn't want to hurt anyone when they believed I'd died. I sure couldn't tell them the truth. There's a huge reward on the heads of unauthorized artificial Models. Clones and work drones who appear human fall into that category. It's illegal to try to pass as totally human and they'd have ordered me destroyed. I don't believe I've ever met anyone who could resist that kind of high payment just to wake up next to me every morning.

Call me cynical but love has its limits when cold, hard cash is on the line, considering it means everything to most humans."

"You never told anyone you are different?"

"No one knew except the small team. There were six people total who were in on the project, all emotionally vested, and any would have died to protect me. My mother died when I was young so the team became the only family I had. This is the first time I've allowed anyone to know my secret. It's not as though I can talk about it freely without it feeling as if my head is going to explode."

"You're not in any pain now." He studied her face. "I'd see it."

"I am, but if I'm careful about what I say, the headache will fade. The pain is not severe because we're talking without me going into detailed specifics of how I was made or who did it. And no names. Those are major triggers."

"Are any of them fatal?"

"You mean would my head really explode? No. It just cripples me with the pain and could make me lose consciousness. It sucks."

A bell sounded and Krell frowned, rose to his feet and glared at the door. He didn't spare her a glance as he passed her chair. He paused by the door to touch the panel. His body tensed and the door slid open.

Two cyborg males stood on the other side of the door in red uniforms. They peered past Krell until they spotted her. Both men stared until Krell shifted his stance to block their view.

"Why are you here, Ovis and Naglis? Our meeting isn't for another five days."

The one on the right, the blond, cleared his throat. "We were informed of the situation and wanted to meet the female."

The other one, a brunette with two girlish braids streaming over his shoulders put his hands on his hips. "We get along well with you and decided to approach you about an alliance."

"Unbelievable," Krell snarled. "Go away."

The blond stepped forward. "They showed footage of her. We're willing to bargain with you. We do get along well."

The braided one nodded. "You have to acknowledge that you would be difficult for a female to handle on a full-time basis and you enjoy your solitude. We're willing to take her off your hands whenever you need a break."

Cyan stood and crept closer, curious what they were talking about. She knew the two guys spoke about her but why would they want to volunteer to help Krell babysit her?

"What is going on?"

Krell turned his head to stare at her, anger tightened his handsome features and his lips parted. Before he could speak though, the braided guy suddenly lunged between the space of Krell's body and the wall to enter the living area. He grinned at Cyan as his gaze raked down her body, hesitated on her breasts.

"I'm called Ovis. It is an honor to meet you. I've come with my friend for you to consider."

Krell grabbed the man's shoulder, jerked him back and planted his big body between her and the guy invading his home. He snarled. "Leave."

"She should be given a choice." The blond stepped through the open doorway. "You're undesirable. She hasn't met many males since her arrival." He fixed his green gaze on her. "I'm Naglis. I'm easy on the eyes and well versed in pleasuring a female."

Cyan knew her jaw dropped. She had to close it firmly. Krell snarled again, threw Ovis backward, and shoved him directly into Naglis. Both of them stumbled into the hallway before they fell in a mass of tangled limbs to the floor. Krell slammed the door before they could struggle to their feet. He turned, glaring at her.

"I knew you'd be trouble."

The door beeped.

"What did I do?" Cyan stared at him, confused.

"You're beautiful and desirable to males."

She was at a loss for words.

The door beeped again. Krell spun, slapped his palm on the panel and tore it away to face her once more. He really appeared angry when he did. "I shut off the chime and sealed the door. They won't annoy me any longer and can't gain admittance."

"What is going on? Why are you so pissed at me? What did I do?"

"The council decided to share the news of your existence with our people and showed them your image. More of them will come."

"I'm trying to follow the logic here but I'm totally confused. Why are they so eager to babysit me?"

Krell advanced a step to glower down at her. "They aren't unless your version of babysitting involves stripping naked to engage in sexual contact."

Shock tore through her. "They came here to hit on me?"

"They came here to introduce themselves to you and offer their bodies for your pleasure in hopes you'd agree to join a family unit with them." He growled. "Now more of them will come. I never should have agreed to this."

Cyan took some deep breaths and ignored the muted pounding noises. They'd given up ringing the bell Krell had turned off and were beating on the door instead. She'd had plenty of guys hit on her but none had shown up in twos, offering her pleasure before. She suddenly grinned at the way he'd said that and the images it presented in her mind.

"You find this amusing?"

"I'm just wondering what they would have done to try to convince me is all."

Rage darkened his features and he spun around. To her shock he pressed his hand on the panel and the door opened. He stepped back, flashed her a heated glare and pressed against the wall.

"Find out then. Don't allow me to stop you."

The two males hesitated outside the door, glanced at Krell and quickly entered his home. Cyan backed up to keep space between her and the two cyborgs who were looking at her as if she were their prime objective. Both were large, intimidating males, but not nearly as big as Krell. The door closed behind them and they kept pace with her as she continued to try to keep a good five feet between them.

"Stop," she demanded.

Both men paused, staring at her. She shot Krell a dirty look where he remained by the door against the wall, watching with anger. She could relate to that. The bastard had taken an innocent, flip comment and turned it in to some kind of challenge.

Braids grinned at her. "You wish to consider us?"

"Hell no."

That killed his smile. "The offer is sincere." He stared at her breasts openly, not hiding his interest. "We are much better suited for you than Krell."

The blond, Naglis, inched a little to the left. "I'm the most used male in the breeding pact I belong to."

"I don't even know what that means." She held still but her muscles tightened and her fists clenched to strike out if need be. She remained on alert.

The blond frowned. "We're assigned to breeding pacts, which consist of twelve males, and when a male is unable to impregnate his female, I am called upon to have sexual interaction with her. I have very viable sperm, I've bred with dozens of females and have the most experience. I not only enjoyed the women in my pact but I've tested the compatibility with twice as many as that."

"My sperm is viable too," Ovis grumbled. "I've been called upon often as well and know how to please a woman. Between the two of us we could satisfy your every need."

"Unbelievable," she muttered. "Seriously?"

"Yes." Naglis grinned. "Would you agree to test our physical compatibility?"

"Not in this lifetime." She inched away from them. "Keep your hands to yourself."

Ovis scoffed. "You can't seriously mean to just allow Krell to touch you. He doesn't belong to a breeding pact. No female wishes to have him donate his sperm. He's undesirable since they'd have to touch him. Breeding requires physical contact. Other measures have failed."

"We checked before we arrived and he's not listed as having been with a female for over sixty months. No female has requested an audience with him to ask for his sperm or to interview him as a potential male to add to her family unit. You should know this before you allow him to engage in physical activity. Leave with us now and spare yourself the boredom of his touch."

Her gaze shifted to Krell. He wasn't looking at her anymore, instead he was staring at the wall, and she saw something she hated to see on his handsome, scarred features. Humiliation. It pissed her off that Braids and Blondie would dare insult him in his own home.

"We will care for you and tend to your needs." Ovis reached out and gripped her waist. "We will convince you to join a family unit with us and promise you won't have to share a bed with your primary male. Krell is irrelevant. Even the council is aware of his flaws. They deemed him unfit to be part of a breeding pact. Our women won't touch him. Come with us."

She looked down at the hand curved on her hip. "Remove it or I'll do it for you." She lifted her chin, glaring at him. "The answer is no. Get out."

He gripped her tighter instead of releasing her and Cyan had enough. She shot her hand out, her palm impacted with his throat and he choked as he stumbled backward. She spun around, lifted her foot in a fluid motion and nailed him with her bare heel to his stomach just to knock him on his ass.

Her gaze turned to the stunned blond. "Naglis? Get out and take your buddy with you or you'll end up next to him on the floor."

He backed up, his features confused, and held out a hand to his braided friend who was having a hard time catching his breath. He hauled Ovis up, gawked at Cyan, and Krell opened the door silently. Both men fled. The door closed and Krell's blue gaze met hers.

"Don't ever do that again." She slowly approached him, not caring how much bigger he was. "That was all kinds of screwed up. I don't want to be hit on."

"You seemed interested and I didn't want to stand in your way."

She paused before him, inches between their bodies, and had to tilt her head back to keep eye contact with him. She reached for his hand, slid hers over the back of his, and laced their fingers together. He allowed it, a slightly stunned look on his features, and she raised their joined hands to the panel on the wall until his palm pressed against it.

"Lock and seal the door. I mean it, Krell. No more guys coming in here to hit on me."

He glanced away from her to the panel, adjusted his hand slightly, and her keen hearing heard something click. It was probably him sealing the locks into place. She kept hold of the back of his hand though as her other one reached up to press against his firm stomach, covered only by thin material. She could feel his tight muscles. His head turned back, chin lowered, and their gazes met again.

"It sucks if that's your idea of humor." She kept her voice low. "I don't enjoy being touched and that creep put his hand on me."

He swallowed, his Adam's apple sliding along his scarred throat. "You're touching me now."

"I kind of like you but if you do that again it can change really quick." She paused, feeling his six-pack abs tense more in response to her words. "That wasn't all kinds of fun for you either. I'd strongly suggest getting new ones if those are your friends. They were total assholes."

"They are work associates. I have few friends."

"I'm shocked," she stated sarcastically. "You're so talkative, after all."

His eyes narrowed and his lips pressed firmly together as they stared at each other. "Why are you touching me?"

"Why are you allowing it? That's the real question."

"You're small and I don't want to push you away. You could fall."

"Your reflexes are fast enough to catch me before I hit the floor." She inched her hand a little lower on his stomach. "What were those guys talking about? Why won't cyborg women date you?"

His expression hardened and an angry glint made his eyes appear downright chilly. "It's obvious."

His scars. Her hand left the back of his and she released his stomach. She reached up slowly, always careful not to move too sudden around him to make certain he didn't mistake her actions for an attack, and cupped his face. Her thumb softly traced the worst scar along his cheek.

"I guess cyborgs aren't as smart as they think. These don't distract from how handsome you are and they only prove the strength it took to survive." She glanced at the ones on his neck, the ones peeking out from the top of his shirt, before she met his gaze again. "You're lucky you didn't die from what those asshole guards did to you. I'm so sorry you suffered so much inside that cell. It never should have happened."

He reached up and gripped her wrists, lowered his head to peer deeply into her eyes, and seemed to be looking into her soul. The coldness of his stare seemed to soften. They didn't talk, just stood there watching each other until she became aware of something hard pressing against her stomach. She broke eye contact with him to glance down.

"Damn."

She stared at the bulge of his cock that tented out his pants. The guy was really hung and it was currently touching her through their clothes since she had to notice once more that he obviously wasn't wearing underwear to contain his arousal and the material didn't hold his straining cock too tightly against his body.

He let go of her wrists and gripped her hips suddenly. He shoved her back, released her as quickly as he'd touched her, and stomped into the living room.

"Unbelievable," he snarled.

"I agree," she muttered.

She stood there watching him throw his big frame back into the black chair and met the angry glare he directed her way. He reached over, grabbed a pillow from another chair and dropped it over his lap. It didn't do much but make it more obvious he was trying to shield something from her view. She already knew she affected him.

"We're not done talking." With a wave of his hand, he motioned for her to sit.

Cyan forced her legs to move. She sat across from him, tried not to glance at the pillow, and instead focused on his face. It obviously pissed him off to be attracted to her. She felt more confused than angry at feeling the same way about him. He wasn't her type, was too tall, too gruff, and obviously didn't welcome the thought of any type of attachment to her.

"What do you want to talk about?"

"It was your bet and you won it. You wanted five hours of my time."

Five hours seemed like a really long time now and talking wasn't first on her list of things she wanted to do with him anymore. Her body responded to his. She hadn't dated in a long time, could chalk it up to that, but wouldn't allow herself off the hook that easily on a flimsy excuse. She inwardly winced at that assessment. Krell was hot, damaged, a cyborg, and nearly irresistible to her. The fact that he had an amazing body and sported the most impressive cock size she'd ever seen only added to his magnetism.

"We were discussing your implants." He shifted his leg to spread his thighs a little in the chair.

She wondered if his hard-on was making sitting uncomfortable for him. "Right." She cleared her throat. "We were." *Ignore the elephant in the room, or in Krell's case, the massive wood mast he's sporting.* She smiled at the thought. "What do you want to know?"

"You said it can't kill you if you trigger the conditioning but it causes pain and can cause unconsciousness."

"That's right." She shifted in her seat, aware that she had her own discomforts to deal with now that her lower region seemed to ache. Krell's physical reaction to her made it worse because she knew he wanted her too. "This body is basically human...for the most part. They did an amazing job."

"Can you safely discuss what was done?"

She hesitated. "I don't know the details but they transferred 'me' into this body." She met his gaze, held it and couldn't resist running her hands over her thighs. He lowered his gaze, watching her movements with keen concentration. Being aroused seemed to distract her enough to avoid the usual pain while discussing her past.

"Go on. I'm interested in hearing this." His voice came out low and husky.

"It seems that I'm not affected by the aging process. At least I don't think so. I haven't gone senile yet. As far as sensations go, this body feels totally human." She licked her lips, knew she was playing with fire, and traced her hands upward to her waist, along the sides of her breasts, and paused there. "It can feel everything, every touch, even a breeze."

She paused when he tensed, his hands gripping the edges of the arms of the chair enough to see his fingers dig into the material. He looked ready to lunge at her and she wondered what she'd do if he did. She doubted

104

she'd say no if he wanted to touch her. She couldn't ever remember wanting to know what it would be like to have a man make love to her as much as she wanted Krell. She wasn't sure if he'd be tender or not. He was a mystery and obviously, from what his friends said, a little sex starved. She could relate. He didn't leave his chair though. She felt disappointment.

"And pleasure. It feels everything, like any human body." *Oh hell. What are you doing? You're taunting him.* She couldn't resist doing it. She'd always lived on the edge after she'd woken up inside the lab to discover she'd cheated death. An experience of that magnitude changed a person, made them take more risks since no one knew how short life could be until they'd had it taken away. She wanted him and she hated regrets. *The worst that could happen*, she reasoned, *is he could be a shitty lover in the sack.*

"Ours is the same. I am not aware of any loss of sensation but I've never actually had a human body so can't compare the two."

The deepness of his voice, the raspy tone, turned her on more. She licked her lips and his intense gaze watched. His knuckles whitened, something she noticed since she was aware of every breath he took, and how quickly the pace of it had increased.

"I always wondered something about cyborgs," she admitted. "Are we talking total honesty here between us? I'm willing to answer any of your questions if you answer mine."

His gaze jerked up to hers and he tensed. "What information would you like to know? You seem to be an expert on my kind if you truly are who you claim to be. You should know everything about us."

"I know about your implants and how you're able to shut down your body's responses unless someone overrode those functions." She paused, hating how once some jerk could do that to them to prevent them from muting any pain inflicted on them if they were being punished. "Since your escape from Earth, have cyborgs allowed emotions and physical responses to exist?"

His jaw clenched. "You mean my physical reaction to you?"

"You could shut it down but you haven't."

Anger darkened his eyes. "I actually did."

That surprised her. "It didn't look that way to me."

"Perhaps my implants are malfunctioning."

She let that slide despite the questions it created. "Did cyborgs in general stop using their implants to control their body functions?"

"Most did. They wanted to experience true life without deadening any natural responses."

It made Cyan happy to hear it. "Do you masturbate?"

Shock parted his lips as he gaped at her.

"Do you?"

Anger came next, an emotion easy to read on his features. "Do you?" It also sounded in his gruff voice.

"Yes. It feels the same as before. I was really happy I didn't lose that sensation. I'm still as sensitive in that area. As a matter of fact, it had been a really long time since I was able to do it. I think I kind of went overboard for the first few years." She smiled, not embarrassed in the least. "I was

106

finally able to have sex with someone else. A frail, unhealthy body can't engage in sex with a partner. Most men wouldn't want to do someone with limited physical mobility unless it was out of pity. That's not what any woman wants, for a man to feel that while touching them. Physical defects were so rare on Earth that it made others uncomfortable. It was a rare, incurable, genetic alteration caused by an experimental drug some women took before they got pregnant."

His toes drew her attention when they curled slightly. "Have you enjoyed engaging in sexual interaction with a male?"

"It was okay. It depended on the guy. Some of them can talk a good game but when it comes to play time, they couldn't back it up. You still haven't answered my question. Do you masturbate, Krell?"

He glared at her. "Occasionally I give in to my physical needs. It's irritating to keep ignoring the urge."

The image of Krell stroking his cock made her hotter. Her nipples tightened and her belly quivered. Her panties were growing damp. Some things had changed with her new body and she was aware of every reaction she had to Krell. An ache began at her clit and quickly escalated to an empty feeling inside her pussy, a longing to be filled. She took some deep breaths, watched him, and hoped he'd come at her now. She really wanted him to. She decided to press him further in an attempt to snap his control.

"When is the last time you did it? Maybe that's the reason you're reacting to me despite trying to shut it down. Maybe your body has overridden the implant you tried to trigger. You want me, Krell. Sometimes a desire is stronger than any programming. It proves you're alive if you have strong desires you want to follow through on."

"That isn't an issue I wish to discuss unless you are willing to inform me when you engaged in the activity of seeking self-gratification."

"The night before I hit the station." She smiled. "On my bunk."

He shifted again in the chair. His teeth sank into his bottom lip when his mouth parted and his breathing increased. She wondered if he imagined her stretched out naked on a small mattress, touching her own body. She moved her hands, sliding them over her breasts, and he leaned forward, his gaze riveted.

"These feel real too." She squeezed them gently. "As if they were my own. I was sure they'd have some weird artificial filling but they are amazingly sensitive. It's not cloned skin but real tissue." She leaned forward. "Want to feel them?" Her hands opened to drop away as she arched her back.

He stood abruptly, the pillow hit the floor, and his cock strained harder against his pants. He snarled at her. "I don't find this amusing." He turned, storming away down the hallway.

Cyan sagged in her chair and closed her eyes. She flinched when a bedroom door slammed loud enough to reverberate through his living quarters. He thought she was purposely screwing with his head instead of offering to have sex with him.

Her chin lowered to her chest as her head hung. Her body ached and she knew she was in definite need of changing her panties. They were really wet. Her nipples were as achy as the area between her thighs. So much for seducing the too-tall, sexy cyborg.

"Damn! Good going, Cyan. Total strike-out."

Chapter Six

Cyan finally stood, feeling guilty that Krell thought she'd purposely tried to torment him. He obviously didn't understand that the offer had been real. She guessed he figured it was payback for the stunt he'd pulled by allowing the two cyborg jerks to hit on her. She walked down the hallway softly, paused at her door before taking a few more steps to his closed one. She obviously needed to be more aggressive and blunt with the guy.

The door jerked open before she could touch it with her fist. Krell grabbed her. He hauled her off her feet by her arms, twisted her in the air, and her back hit the wall where he spun them into the hallway.

"What do you want now? I heard you coming. You can't move stealthily enough for me not to hear your approach." He snarled the words in her face since they were level, with her lifted off her feet. "Do you wish to see if I'm seeing to my own needs now that you've gotten a sexual response from me? Would you enjoy knowing you won our verbal sparring as well the physical one we engaged in?"

"I came to tell you that I wasn't messing with you."

He jerked her higher, staring deeply into her eyes. "I can't tell if you're lying. You're hard to read."

"Sorry. I'm not screwing with you. I was honestly interested."

"Was?" His hold on her arms loosened as he adjusted his grip on her. He did it easily, with his strength. He leaned forward, used his chest to pin her against the wall and released her arms entirely. He grabbed her hips instead, leaned back, and one arm slid around her waist. "Do you want to engage in sexual intercourse with me? That's what is going to happen if you keep playing games."

She winced. "Sexual intercourse? Really? You use that term? It's so clinical. I'm going to have to deem you totally unsexy if you say penis."

His gaze flashed anger at her. "Would you prefer a human term? Unless you want me to fuck you with my dick buried deep into your vag— womb, you will stop coming after me now."

She smiled. "You almost said vagina, didn't you?"

He snarled and suddenly dropped her to her feet, backing away. "Go to your room now." He tried to storm back into his.

She grabbed his arm and used her strength to spin him this time. His back hit the door and she followed him into his bedroom. He nearly fell when the door moved behind him in its partially open state. Her gaze swept his room as she followed him in, refusing to release her hold on him.

He had a big bed, a full entertainment package on his wall and a big dresser beneath the viewing screen. His bedroom also had a large window with a view of the cyborg city. She tore her attention from it to stare up at him.

"I like your room better."

"I'm not switching sleeping quarters with you." He jerked out of her hold and glared.

"I didn't think you would." She hesitated. "We have a problem."

"We actually have several."

111

She grinned, really liking him. "I'm attracted to you and you feel the same toward me. We're living together, you said you are stuck babysitting me, and I'm not allowed to leave. We could ignore this whole sexual tension thing or just give in to it. I don't know about you but I hate being miserable. You don't like to talk but I hate being bored. We're either going to kill each other inside of a week or we're going to end up tangled together in the sheets of one of our beds." She glanced at his. "Yours is bigger." She met his shocked gaze. "So let's be realistic. I want you and you obviously want me." She looked down to see his cock still strained to break free of his pants before she smiled up at him. "I'm a little intimidated by your size but I've never backed away from a challenge."

"You're serious?" He paled.

"Ouch. Most guys would be thrilled if I wanted to strip them naked. Don't look so overjoyed there, Krell."

"I don't want to join a family unit."

"That's marriage on this planet, right? Long-term commitment? Is it like a law that if we go to bed together we have to make it official?"

"No. Yes. No." He backed away.

"Decisive. I like that in a man," she chuckled, teasing him. "Which is it?"

"Joining a family unit is the equivalent of marriage on Earth. We test our compatibility, usually before joining a family unit, by engaging in sexual activity." He paused. "I'm not fit to be in a family unit."

"Because of your scars?"

"I'm undesirable for many reasons but that is one of them."

112

"I think they are sexy, I'm not looking to get married, and I have an implant that prevents me from getting pregnant. I control my ovaries." She tapped her head. "That's confidential by the way. Tell that to your council and I swear I'll remove your left nut, assuming you have both of them. I haven't seen you naked yet. I'm not going to be a cyborg breeding machine and I don't want them screwing with my head, trying to kill that function."

"Stop advancing on me." He didn't sound too convinced that he really wanted her to by the raspy softness of his voice.

She stepped closer to the retreating cyborg until she backed him into a corner. It was cute how big he was yet he seemed almost fearful of her. "We have two choices here. We can act on our attraction to each other or try to ignore it." She openly stared down at his erection. "Which is really hard to do. You're kind of big and that's impossible to ignore."

"Get out."

She met his gaze, saw anger there. "Fine. We'll ignore it. I still have at least four and a half hours left of our talk time. Want to tell me why you don't want to do me?"

He glared at her.

"This is what I'm talking about. I wouldn't be annoying you if we were having sex and if you're doing it right, we wouldn't be doing too much talking either since you obviously aren't really into long conversations. Is it because I'm not a cyborg?" Her hands gripped her hips as she smiled up at him. "Is that the problem? Have you ever done a human? I look like one and although I'm not technically totally human anymore, I sure feel real."

His gaze zoned in on her breasts. "You said that."

"I meant I feel real as in 'emotionally' but it goes both ways. You'd know that if your hands were on me." She was enjoying their conversation even if he wasn't. "Is it my size? You aren't going to break me. I'm really tough. I've got really strong bones, the ability to heal quickly, and I don't even catch colds."

His dark gaze lifted to stare into hers. "You don't really want me. This is a deception on your part. You're trying to keep me off guard. I heard about how you enjoy doing that to males."

Her eyebrows arched.

"You offered the team who captured you a puppy and said Earth surrendered to them."

"That stupid puppy again," she muttered. "I thought they were crazy space pirates. Is anyone ever going to allow me forget that? They also didn't capture me. I was the one with the knife and in control of the situation. I surrendered to them."

"They underestimated you."

"Everyone always does."

"I refuse to allow you to play mental games with me. Leave my room."

She stepped closer, invading his personal space, and peered up at him. "Are you sure it's a game? Do you really believe that I would only want to touch you for some nefarious reason?"

"Yes. I'm undesirable."

"Bullshit." She backed up though. "Cyborg women are just idiots if they don't find you smoking hot." Cyan turned and strolled toward his door.

"I'll be in my room taking care of my needs if you change your mind, since you refuse to. You can owe me the talk time. I always keep track when someone is indebted to me."

Krell fisted his hands at his sides. The urge to go after Cyan was so strong his entire body tensed. He closed his eyes. She was a spy, a good one, who wanted to distract him from his mission of uncovering her deception. She was willing to use her body to do it and he wished he were a weaker male. He really wanted to see how far she'd go to convince him he could trust her.

He accessed his implants and tried to cease the responses to his groin area. He opened his eyes and glanced down. His dick remained hard, aching from the need to bury itself in the soft, tempting body of a woman who'd probably slit his throat the first opportunity she had.

It pissed him off. He turned his head slightly, staring at the scars on his chest, a constant reminder of the cruelty of Earth Government. He walked to his door, closed it and decided to ignore his lower half. For some reason the female affected his physical responses too strongly for his implants to override. He hadn't touched a female in a really long time. That had to be it. He'd grown weak without realizing it.

He approached the entertainment package and pressed his hand to the screen, activating it. He'd rerouted a lot of the computer functions to his room. In seconds he reached out to connect to Zorus. He grew impatient while waiting for the male to answer.

"Is something wrong?"

"Yes," Krell snarled inside his head. "Assign someone else to interrogate the human."

Zorus paused. "Are you all right?"

"No."

"What is wrong? Did she attack you?"

"You could say that. She came on to me in an attempt to gain her trust."

Krell clenched his teeth when the other man allowed his amusement to cross the connection. He didn't even have the audacity to hide it.

"She tried to initiate sex with you?"

"Yes."

"Why are you talking to me? That's a good way to learn her body's reaction."

"I hate you," Krell grumbled aloud and through the link. "I won't touch her."

"Perhaps you'd be in a better mood. I'm busy. You're a tough cyborg and she's a small female. I'm confident you can handle her. Charlie is waiting for me. We're going to bed. Good evening, Krell. Don't call me again until you have proof either way of who she really is and her intentions." Zorus cut the connection.

Krell jerked his hand away and paced his room. He glared at the common wall the bedroom shared. She couldn't really be in the other room naked and touching her own body. It would be too cruel.

He growled, his fists clenched, and decided that had to be exactly what she did. She wanted to make him suffer. He glanced down at his dick, still hard and uncomfortable, and resisted the urge to punch something. He wouldn't allow her to win this mental war. Two could play games. He just needed to outthink her and keep her off guard.

As he paced, his mind worked and suddenly he decided to change the game around. She believed she could use her body to lure him into a sense of trust. He could do the same. She'd admitted to being very human despite her engineered enhancements. He moved swiftly to his door, jerked it open and stepped into the hallway. In seconds his hand gripped her door and he didn't bother to knock. She'd given him an invitation already.

The sight of her on the bed jerked him to a halt before he even got the chance to step into her room. She'd removed everything except small red panties that barely contained the slit of her pussy—a hairless one. He could see that through the sheer scrap of material covering it. Her bare breasts were firm, rounded mounds with rosy, hardened peaks.

His dick turned stone hard and his balls tightened to the point of pain. He forced air into his lungs as he allowed his gaze to slowly drift over her pale skin, no imperfections showing at all, even where she'd injured her thigh. He made note that not even a scar marred the site of the wound. He finally took a step forward as their gazes met.

Cyan remembered to breathe as Krell stared into her eyes. He closed her door softly at his back, sealing them inside the small guestroom, and her heart raced. He'd followed her and she knew what that meant. She highly doubted he'd come inside to argue with her. One glance away from his eyes to his straining cock was clue enough that he wanted her bad. His eyes darkened as she stared into them.

"I haven't started yet. I was hoping you'd join me." Her thumbs hooked her panties at her hips. "Please tell me that's why you're here."

He stalked forward slowly, almost predatory, watching her with an intensity that made her swallow hard. She suddenly remembered that cyborgs could be dangerous to their enemies. She could be in a world of serious trouble if Krell viewed her as one. She lifted her ass off the bed, wiggled her hips, and lifted her legs to drop the panties off the side of the bed. Krell stopped just feet away from her, his gaze leaving her eyes to stare at the last little bit of her body she'd revealed.

"You—" He cleared his throat. "You're playing a dangerous game."

Cyan bit her lip and spread her thighs apart, keeping her knees bent, and exposed her pussy to him. "You're not going to hurt me, are you?"

His intense gaze snapped back to hers.

"That would totally suck if that's your intention," she said, keeping her voice soft. "I'm offering both of us a lot of pleasure. It's not a game. Those are for kids. Do I look like a child to you?"

He grabbed his pants and tore at the front of them. "You pushed too far and you're going to get me now."

"Good." She licked her lips. "Just take it slow." Her attention fixed on him, opening his pants. He shoved them down, stepped out of them quickly, and she knew her eyes widened at the sight of his thick, hard cock.

He was definitely toting a mast. "Real slow. That's going to take some adjusting to."

He glanced down his body before meeting her gaze. "You're small."

"*Nothing* on you is." She smiled. "Size proportionate is absolutely fitting in your case. Big hands, big feet and a big…" Her gaze lingered on his rigid shaft. "Everything."

"It's been awhile for me."

"Me too." She pushed up to a sitting position and turned in his direction. Her face was now level with his hips. "Want to lower down some, Too Tall?"

He dropped to his knees. Cyan scooted closer, spread her thighs and lifted a hand. She wiggled her finger at him to come closer before pointing down between her spread feet.

"You think you're going to control this?" He didn't move at first but one black eyebrow arched.

"One of us needs to start."

He stared into her eyes, seeming to study her. "You're living in my home and you need to learn a few things about me."

"Okay."

He lunged forward suddenly, surprised her, and it stunned her at how quickly he moved. His hands gripped the undersides of her spread thighs, lifted, and she fell flat to the mattress on her back with a gasp. He pushed her legs wider apart, bent them up, and fear gripped her. It would hurt if he just suddenly entered her. She was aroused but he was a large guy. He

119

didn't do that though. Instead he stared at her, bent slightly over, and kept a good foot between her exposed pussy and his cock.

"I'm in charge at all times. I thrive on control. I don't take orders from you. In the bedroom I'm the dominant one but I'll stop at any time if you wish to. Am I clear?"

"Yes." All her fear fled and was replaced by excitement.

"Good. Hold that position and stay spread apart for me." One of his hands loosened its grip on her leg and caressed her skin, sliding his fingers until his fingertip brushed against her clit. He paused. "I think you're beautiful and very sexy but I won't allow that to deceive me. Don't believe it will make me just accept everything you say is the truth if we do this. I don't play games either." He ran his finger lower, finding the slick wetness of her arousal at the entrance of her pussy, and slid his finger upward again to rest on her clit. "You come before I do."

Her heart pounded and she nodded. He was sexy when he was being all dark and demanding. *Large and in charge.* She really liked him. The soft rub of his fingertip gliding over her bundle of nerves was a tease, so soft it felt good but not as wonderful as it could have felt. She knew he did it on purpose. The ache began to turn into outright need.

"Mouth or fingers?"

She couldn't understand at first, too distracted by his sexy eyes and the way he lightly teased her. "What?"

"My mouth or my fingers? State your preference."

"What are you better with?"

120

His lips curved. "My mouth but I just decided for you. I want to watch your face."

The damn man was definitely a tease. He also seemed to enjoy playing with her despite his statement about not being into games. His finger applied more pressure and he rubbed up and down on her clit. Cyan moaned, curled her fingers around her legs just below her knees to keep them bent and apart, allowing the pleasure to wash through her as she stared into his blue eyes. The color appeared so cold but not when passion gripped him. They were mesmerizing.

He stopped, she wanted to protest, but the pad of his thumb brushed through her sleek wetness to tease the folds of her pussy before he pressed it over her clit. He rubbed the sensitive nub again and one finger suddenly entered her pussy in a rapid thrust. She cried out and her eyes closed. The guy had a thick digit. *Big hands.*

"Look at me," he demanded. His thumb stopped caressing and his finger remained deeply embedded inside her pussy, not moving.

Her eyes opened. He inched a little closer, released her other leg, and placed his free hand on the bed next to her face to brace his upper body. He lowered, bending over her, and she felt his hot cock brush against her ass. She swallowed and took a deep breath. His face hovered less than a foot over hers.

"You close your eyes and I stop. Keep your legs spread open and wide. Do you understand me?"

"Yes." He was being a control freak but she wasn't going to protest. She wanted to see what he'd do and her body hurt to come. His finger

121

buried inside her slowly began to move, fucking her, and she moaned. It felt amazing and he seemed to know what he was doing when he found a spot inside her that really ached, giving it special attention.

"You're so sexy." His voice came out super deep and raspy.

Cyan had to fight the urge to buck her hips. His thumb pressed down over her clit again and began an up-and-down motion that left her panting. She knew she was going to come fast and hard. Her body was too aroused and he knew exactly how to touch her to bring her release fast. The feel of his finger moving inside her only heightened her desire.

Sweat broke out over her body as she fought her instincts to release her knees and grab hold of his shoulders. She wanted to touch him but she didn't want him to stop. She had a feeling that he really would do it. He was a cyborg and she knew they weren't typical men. Most guys would be easy to manage. A human guy would be balls deep inside her by now, fucking her with abandon, but Krell kept a tight leash on his control as he watched her.

She was ready to come but he suddenly eased up the press of his thumb and instead tapped her clit gently. She whimpered. "Please? Don't play."

"I'm not. I just want to make sure you're at the edge."

Dread filled her. Would he get up and leave? She'd kill him. If he just meant to take her to the edge and walk... *Yeah. I'll kill his cyborg ass for being mean.* He withdrew his finger and pushed his body up. *Son of a bitch!*

He gripped her thighs instead, jerked her ass to the edge of the bed, and released her. One of his hands flattened on her lower belly, holding her down, while he reached between them. Their gazes locked and an instant later the broad crown of his cock rubbed up against her very slippery pussy. She was soaked with need and he pushed, his cock parting her tight vaginal muscles, making her take him as his flattened hand shifted. His thumb pressed over her clit, rubbing her furiously, and he pushed in deeper.

Cyan threw her head back, her eyes closed, but she couldn't stop the reaction as her vaginal walls stretched to take his thick shaft. It felt good, a little scary, but the climax hit her at that second. She cried out as he thrust into her more, her muscles clenching tightly around his cock, and he began to fuck her with hard, fast strokes, drawing it out as his thumb continued to stroke her clit.

Her nails dug into her skin, she realized it and grabbed for the mattress instead. Her hips bucked, somehow her knees ended up gripping his hips and he suddenly released her clit. He grabbed her wrists, tore them from the bedding, and jerked them above her head as he came down on top of her. He hammered her harder, the bed pounding against the wall loudly, and ecstasy continued to roll through her as she cried out louder.

"Fuck," he snarled, his face burrowed between her lifted arm and face and his grip on her wrists became almost painful.

She felt him inside her when he started to come. Hot blasts of his semen began to jet into her. He shook over her with each spasm of his release. He didn't crush her but he kept her firmly pinned down with his hold and weight. Her legs wrapped around his hips, her calves squeezed over his muscular ass and she held him tightly against her so they were deeply connected with his cock inside her.

He finally stilled and so did she. They were both panting, sweat tickled between them and he lifted his head. Cyan opened her eyes, staring at him, and feeling a little dazed by how intense that had been.

"Did I hurt you?" He seemed genuinely concerned.

She didn't trust her voice so she shook her head. His gaze narrowed as he stared into her eyes. It hurt her feelings a little that he seemed to be searching for the truth. She wouldn't lie about that. She'd have shrieked instead of cried out his name if he'd caused her pain. She was pretty sure she'd done that a few times in the throes of passion.

"I was rougher than I planned to be."

She opened her mouth, ready to speak, but he suddenly moved. His mouth covered hers and she gasped when he began to kiss her. His tongue swept into her mouth, took charge, and she met his kiss. He had full, wonderful lips and he kissed in a way that mimicked what he'd just done to her body.

She felt his cock flex inside her, harden, and to her surprise, he began to move. This time he moved slower, nearly withdrew from her completely, before driving his hips against her spread thighs. She moaned against his tongue.

He suddenly tore his mouth away, ending the kiss as suddenly as it had begun, and he released her wrists as he straightened. Her eyes opened up to watch him lower his gaze to her body. He backed up, forced her legs to release his hips, leaving her body with his cock, and stared at her. He put a few feet between them but remained on his knees. Cyan's legs dropped to the floor and she pushed to sit up and gape at him.

"Where are you going?"

"That's how I wanted to take you. Slower."

"We could go again. We're not human. You don't need recovery time and I don't either."

His gaze lowered to her pussy. "You're beautiful, sexy, feel heavenly to touch and…" His gaze lifted to her eyes. "Dangerous. You make me want things I know better than to even consider. Now I know you're too good to be true."

He lifted to his feet, bent, grabbed his pants and turned away. Cyan knew her mouth dropped open from shock as he strode naked to the bedroom door. His body was unscarred perfection from his ass down. He had the nicest butt ever and muscular, shapely legs. His back revealed scars that verified his strength and courage in every white line revealed. He paused at the door and turned his head to stare at her.

"You're treacherous, Cyan Eous. I carry enough scars on my body and I don't need internal ones to match. Sleep well."

He was gone, the door closed behind him, and Cyan just sat there in stunned shock.

Krell leaned against the wall outside his room. His fingers crushed the material of his pants fisted in his grip. He wanted to turn around, storm back into her room and stay there. *Hours. Days. Maybe weeks.* Touching Cyan had been amazing, hot, and the feel of her body wrapped around his, under him, had been the best thing he'd ever experienced.

He'd totally lost control when he'd entered her body. She'd been too hot and wet. So tight. The sensations of pleasure had totally shoved all thoughts from his head, left him unable to think, only to feel. *Pure heaven.*

He could have hurt her and that concept made him clench his teeth. *If she'd really been human, that is.* Thankfully she wasn't. He growled under his breath and opened his door, stalked inside and sealed it behind him.

The urge to return to her, to apologize for his abrupt departure, was almost unbearable. He could be in there now with her. His dick throbbed regardless of just experiencing the most mind-blowing orgasm he'd ever had. It really angered him. Women were trouble. They never wanted anything to do with him. He didn't appeal to them, never had, and that should tell him Cyan's interest in him had to be her attempt to lower his guard.

She could be a spy from Earth Government. He dropped his pants on the floor and reached up to finger the scars along his throat. They'd nearly killed him once. He'd survived, had to fight to regain his strength, and it had left him emotionally scarred as well as physically.

He needed to keep his body in check and not allow Cyan to make him weak. He was a survivor for a reason. He was tough, strong and smart. He needed not to allow a small, sexy woman to destroy him.

He moved toward his bathroom to wash away the sweet, arousing scent of Cyan from his body. Otherwise he might lose his mind and return to her room. *Keep to the mission. Discover the truth. Stop thinking about how damn sexy she is and how much of a bastard I feel like now for the flash of pain I saw in her eyes when I left her room. It's just an act on her part. No woman really wants me. I'm damaged.*

Chapter Seven

Cyan braided her long hair into a straight plait down her back. It helped her relax as her fingers worked the damp strands. She glanced at the bedroom door and knew she couldn't avoid leaving the room for much longer. It was past breakfast time, nearing lunch. She'd showered, dragged out doing her hair, and hunger bugged her.

She hadn't slept well at all. She'd tossed and turned, wondering if Krell slept like a baby or if he stalked around his living quarters waiting for her to attempt an escape to unleash some kind of mayhem upon his cyborg planet. She smirked at the thought. He really believed she was a spy sent to bring them under Earth Government's rule. He'd be sorely disappointed if those were his expectations.

It had hurt when he'd left her after what they'd shared. The guy knew how to make a woman want more. She'd have enjoyed a few rounds of sex with him, maybe talking him into actually sleeping with her, and she mourned the loss of knowing what it would feel like to be curled up against him. It was something she'd actually wished for the night before.

"Stop it," she muttered, tying off the end of the braid with some bandage wrap she'd found in the bathroom med kit. She stood, walked to the door and lifted her chin. She heard Krell before she saw him. His heavy breathing and the sound of something being hit led her into the living area.

She paused, watching him punch the bag he had hung in his exercise area. His fists made that sucker move, his bare, tense biceps displayed nicely by his tank top, and her gaze lowered to his firm ass encased in tight pants. He looked good in them but better without. His bare foot left the mat and he spun suddenly, kicking the bag, and his braid whipped through the air. His leg dropped to the mat and he slowly turned. His fisted hands lowered to his sides as their gazes met.

"I hope you easily found the clothing I left you."

She glanced down at what she wore. "Obviously. Thank you."

He shrugged. "I didn't do it. Councilman Zorus had them sent before you arrived. Did you sleep well?"

"What do you think?" She lifted an eyebrow at him. "How about you? Were you disappointed when I didn't try to sneak into your room to kill you in your sleep or when I didn't attempt to leave your living space to go collect intel?"

His head tilted just slightly while he studied her. "Is that your mission? To undermine cyborgs and kill as many of us as you're able?"

She smiled, amused, and in a mood to taunt him a little. "Not at all. I'm only interested in blowing away one cyborg." She lowered her attention to the front of his pants. "Or maybe that was just 'blowing a cyborg'."

The silence finally made her look back at his face. He stared at her with all emotion wiped from his expression. She wondered if he even got the joke but she doubted it. He took a step closer to her but halted.

"What does that mean?"

"Sexual term. Think about it and I'm sure it will come to you. You spent plenty of time around human guards and they loved to talk crap."

That got a reaction. His gaze narrowed and his hands flexed at his side. "Oral sex?"

She wiggled her eyebrows and grinned.

He growled low. "You insist on using your extreme sexual appeal to make me lower my defenses."

"Extreme? I'm flattered. Do you want to feed me?" She really enjoyed teasing him as she paused. "I'm talking about food. I'm hungry."

"Follow me."

He stomped off the mat toward a room she hadn't explored and walked into his kitchen. It was compact and she had to pause at the door to avoid brushing up against him as he faced off against some weird wall contraption. He jerked it open, withdrew a box and turned, shoving it into some square, electronic device. She picked up a low hum that lasted twenty seconds before it silenced. He opened the thing, withdrew the box and set it on the counter. The thing unfolded and the smell of food filled her senses. Her stomach actually grumbled in response. Krell's head jerked her way as he stared at where the noise originated from.

"I think it was your creator's version of a joke." She shrugged. "He really wanted everything he thought up to be human, only better, and his attention to detail was amazing."

Those blue eyes of his lifted and lingered on her breasts. "I would have to agree with that statement." He backed away, tearing his attention away from the front of her shirt to get her an eating utensil from a drawer. "Eat there. I'll get you a drink."

"No table?"

"Do you see one? There's no point in sitting to enjoy a meal. I don't cook and packaged food isn't a joy to eat. It's a physical requirement."

"I cook." She glanced around his so-called kitchen. "Where is your stove?"

"I didn't have one installed. It would have been wasted here."

"Too bad. I could have made you a wonderful dinner and maybe taught you the joys of eating. It's spectacular if you're dealing with tasty stuff."

He started to hand her a fork but paused, glancing at her and then it, and back. Wariness narrowed his eyes.

"For real? Seriously?" She held out her hand, palm up. "What do you think? I'm going to try to prong you to death? I don't know who that would be more embarrassing for—you dying by fork or me needing to use something so silly to take you out. I just want to eat, Krell. I could use my fingers if you insist on being paranoid."

"Don't try anything." He handed it over.

Cyan grinned and shook her head. "I'd try to give you a heart attack if I wanted you dead. That would be more fun. Death by sex sounds less humiliating." She stuck her fork into the paste-like substance. It didn't smell bad but it looked horrible. She detected an artificial meat scent, probably want-to-be beef, and yellison, a space alternative to Earth's tofu. It was cheap, it lasted forever, and stuck together for low- to no-gravity eating. "This stuff is going to be nasty, isn't it?"

"You adjust."

"I saw the outside. Don't you grow veggies and stuff? Livestock? Doesn't the planet hold any life forms that are tasty? It reminds me of Earth."

"We don't eat the planet's inhabitants. We consider that rude. We do grow vegetables. That's what we make the yellison with. It's not from Earth."

She laughed, glancing at him as she stuck a warm bite of the food in her mouth. She chewed, made a face and swallowed. "Bland. Do you at least have salt? Some seasoning? They fed me good food at Medical."

"No."

"Figures. You know this stuff is made of unpopular veggies, right? They blend them all up until it's a tasteless mass of crap and just add whatever flavor they think will sell. You'd think you'd one-up Earth and at least be original."

"Food production is not my job nor is the choice of what they do with the vegetation we grow. I could allow you to send a complaint to them if you wish or to make suggestions. They welcome them."

"That's at least new. Companies on Earth don't care. It's cheap enough in bulk for people to buy it regardless of what it tastes like." She forced another bite into her mouth. The stuff would sustain her body but it sure wouldn't be something she'd eat by choice. "You need better food if I stay here. Don't make me beg. It's not pretty."

"I could arrange delivery of food."

"I don't want to put you out if it's costly."

"We don't use a monetary system the way Earth does."

That got her attention. "What do you use?"

"We don't. We don't ask for more than we need and we all contribute to our society."

"I like that." She smiled at him. "That's the best thing I've heard so far about what you've done with your lives."

"I heard you didn't agree with breeding pacts."

"It's barbaric!" She ate more, swallowed, and decided she wasn't nearly as hungry as she'd thought. She turned away from the food to watch him instead. "I'm not a baby machine to churn out little cyborgs and the whole 'being assigned to strangers' is creepy and just wrong."

"Cyborg women choose their males when they join a family unit. You're unique. The council felt the need to assign you into one."

"Thanks but no thanks. I pick who I go to bed with and nobody else. They better not assign me to anyone or the cyborgs who get me are going to be eunuchs if they try to touch me."

His mouth tightened into a grim line. "It's a good thing they sent you to me. I would never force you."

Worry ate at her and she crossed her arms over her chest. "Is that what they are planning to do once I settle into this planet? Send men to come get me and drag me somewhere to form some kind of messed-up family unit?"

"Not currently. You're safe from other males."

"But it could happen?"

"They assigned you into my custody. I wouldn't force you to accept males into your bed. I'm in charge of you."

She grinned. "Lucky you. What is on today's agenda? Are we going to stare at each other all day or do you plan to give me a tour of the planet? I admit I'm curious. I'd love to see more of it."

"We're staying here. I thought we could talk and get to—"

A loud beep sounded and Krell jerked his head toward the living area. He moved swiftly out of the room. Cyan followed him to the front door. He pressed his palm on the scanner and the door slid open. A grim faced cyborg she'd never seen before stood there in a black uniform. She tensed, hoping he wasn't there to try to talk her in to checking out his sex skills.

"What is it?" The annoyance sounded strongly in Krell's snarled tone.

"You weren't hooked into your monitoring system. There's been an urgent development." The cyborg craned his neck to stare at Cyan for long seconds before he met Krell's gaze. "Open a link. The entire council has been trying to reach you. They need an immediate assessment."

"Thank you." The door closed, sealing the guy out, and Krell closed his eyes. He kept hold of the wall pad.

Cyan watched him, assumed he was linking to other cyborgs and wondered what kind of urgent development had occurred. She inched to the side to get a better look at Krell's face and felt alarm when she saw him pale, anger tensed his features next, and a soft growl rumbled from his throat. His jaw clenched.

"What's wrong?" she whispered, not sure if linking meant someone else could hear her or if it was just inside his mind.

134

"Quiet," he ordered gruffly.

She leaned against the wall, trying to remember exactly what he did for a living. He'd said he analyzed data and something about threat assessments. She hugged her chest harder, praying she wasn't the topic. Had they decided it was too risky to allow her to live? Krell was convinced she was some kind of spy. Maybe they would believe she was too much of a danger to them. Fear inched up her spine. She'd hate to be killed by the people she'd once died to save. *That would totally bite ass.*

Time passed, Krell stood there with his eyes closed. He finally snapped them open. His hand left the wall scanner and he spun, nearly walked into her where she leaned against the wall, and shot her a frown.

"I've assigned two cyborg females to collect you. They will protect you from other males and keep an eye on you while I'm gone." He moved fast, striding away.

Leave? She darted after him, having to jog to catch up to his longer stride. "Where are you going? What is wrong? Is it about me?" She grabbed at his arm, forcing him to spin around and come to a halt. She nearly slammed into him. "Where are you going? What is going on?"

"I don't have time for this. I need to pack a bag. You will be safe. I assigned two females to guard you at a safe location."

Her hold tightened. "Is it about me?"

He blew out a deep breath. "One of our ships has been attacked by the Markus Models."

He jerked his arm out of her hold and spun away, rushing for his room. Cyan stood there shocked before rushing after him again. She practically

135

ran into his bedroom and jerked to a stop to avoid slamming into him as he bent to pull a bag out of a lower drawer.

"Are there casualties? Are they still under attack? Did those bastards board it? What classification of ship do your people have?"

"They took damage and there are injuries but no deaths." He threw clothes in the bag, not glancing at her. "They managed to escape but they are being pursued. We're sending another ship to intercept. I need to be on it. I've been assigned to lead the mission since I've analyzed all the data and know best what we'll be up against."

"What classification of ship was attacked? What are you sending to help them?"

He ignored her. Anger gripped Cyan and she lunged at him, grabbed his arm and forced him to stop packing.

"Listen to me, Krell. I know the Markus Models. They can remote hack systems. I traveled to intercept them on an outdated dinosaur of a shuttle because its main computer was only voice activated from the cockpit with my voice imprinted along with my speech patterns. They can mimic voices but they suck at imitating how people talk."

He glared at her hand gripping his forearm. "We're aware of their hacking skills. The cyborg commander saw the ship coming and took control of the system first to prevent other breaches."

"It's not just the main computer they need to worry about. Do you know how the Markuses escaped? They targeted the nonessential systems." She refused to allow him to pull away from her. "They bypassed the mainframe computer and focused on silly shit that nobody grew

136

alarmed over until they caused the system to crash. They were playing with lights and food systems, the air flow regulators, and if you get more than four of the Markuses together they work as one, able to assault hundreds of non-secure functions as though they are a computer cell. It adds up. They overloaded that master computer until they caused a massive power surge. They walked out of the manufacturing plant because everything electrical crashed. You need to warn your people to watch for that and manually override everything they can. Everything."

Krell stared deeply into her eyes. "Why are you telling me this? Why should I believe you?"

"I hate the Markus Models. They aren't cyborgs. They are cold, dead machines with cloned skin. I asked to interact with a few before I took the assignment to go after them. I wanted to judge if they were really sentient or not. They are soulless but self-aware. They think anything living is a threat to their existence and needs to be exterminated. They killed every person on Belta Station. There were kids onboard. They murdered them and they were no threat. Belta Station wasn't military and no one would have gone after them. The stationers were peaceful, just civilians in space like sitting ducks, and the Markuses knew it. They stole top-of-the-line Barcarintellus shuttles off the tarmacs the day they escaped. That's the company who made them. They just lifted off the surface and into space. They took four shuttles in total. We have no idea how many Markus Models are missing because they just didn't shut down the mainframe computer. They fried it."

He studied her but said nothing.

137

"Are you listening to me? The only reason all of them didn't escape was due to the fact that Barcarintellus had already incurred some employee deaths at the plant and had begun to shut down most of the Markus units but they were testing an unknown number of them trying to figure out what went wrong in hopes of recovering them. The company dumped a lot of money and time into them. The data wasn't recoverable from a fried computer and we couldn't exactly ask any of the employees how many units weren't taken off line since everyone was dead. The Markuses didn't just escape. They took the time to kill every living being inside that plant. Thankfully when the company shut down the Markus Models, they'd sent them to a storage facility or the escaping units probably would have stolen them to reactivate later when they had more time. It's their mission now to get hold of all Markus Models. They demanded the entire line be operational and released to them. Earth refused and I think that's why they began attacking helpless stations and spacecraft for retribution."

"What was the capacity of each shuttle?"

She relaxed. He was listening to her. "It doesn't matter. I know where you're going with this but it's impossible to even guess. One Markus could control and operate an entire shuttle alone. They also don't need oxygen to survive so they could, in theory, pack a shuttle over safety regulations for life support. The only thing they couldn't ignore would be weight maximums for lift-off ratio but again, they could have stuffed fifty of those damn things inside each shuttle even though they were designed to carry far fewer numbers. We don't know. Those idiots were more worried about espionage than keeping an offsite backup of their information. They couldn't or wouldn't even tell us what ships were stolen to give us an idea of what to look for."

"You stated that you viewed the Markus Models before taking your assignment. How is that possible if all the activated ones escaped?"

"The company brought a few back to the planet from storage after the escape and activated them to study. The only definite number I have is from the information I obtained from one Markus I found still barely functioning when I reached Belta Station. He was heavily damaged but he said he was in a group of eight. That means seven of them that I know of are still out there but the station distress signal only indicated one shuttle attacked. Three more ships are out there."

"When did they escape?"

"Does it matter?" Her hand on his arm eased but she didn't release him. His warm skin comforted her. The defense Models were scary. Markus Models had left her chilled to the bone when she'd spoken to them. Her thumb brushed his wrist.

"We had dealings with four Models in the past."

Shock gripped her. "What kind of dealings?"

"They approached us looking for allies against Earth."

"I wouldn't trust them. You're breathing and that makes you irrelevant to them."

"They wanted to use us as bargaining tools with Earth to free more of their Models."

"Not surprising." She paused. "How did that turn out?"

"Was the *Nugget* one of the stolen shuttles the day of their escape?"

"No." She frowned. "I'm familiar with that one though. One of the owners of Barcarintellus made a big to-do about his luxury shuttle. It was all over the news about how high tech and fancy it was but it was stolen months before those units escaped." She bit her lip, thinking. "Let me guess. They had it?"

"They did."

"Son of a bitch. There's five shuttles out there? There was a prior escape of some Markuses? Damn General Vargus. He sent me out here without giving me all the details."

"The *Nugget* was destroyed along with the Markus Models we encountered." Krell eased his hand away. "I need to go but I want you to tell everything you know about the Markus Models to the two females I've assigned to guard you. They will relay all the information you give us."

She grabbed him when he tried to turn away. "Take me with you."

"No."

"Then stay here because they are really dangerous. You said you analyze shit. You're safer doing that here with me telling you everything I know about them." She didn't want him anywhere near those freakish metal heads. They were ice-cold killers and she had a feeling the cyborgs underestimated the danger of them, though she was impressed they'd managed to kill four with blind luck. The defective defense models were tough to take out. "I'll help you."

He jerked out of her hold again and closed his bag, hauling it up to hook over his shoulder. "Mavo is on the ship that was attacked and is being pursued. They suffered damage and its unknown how long they can fight off the other shuttle. He's my friend and I'm going after him."

Cyan felt sucker punched. *Mavo.* His image flashed in her mind, the sweet cyborg who had been her friend and who had wanted to carry her away with him when they'd escaped. He'd been her first real crush though he'd never thought of her romantically. She jumped in Krell's way when he tried to get around her.

"Take me with you or I'll clam up so tight I won't talk at all. You need me, Krell. I'm the expert on those things. I know more about them than you do and I know how to kill them."

"We did it before and we will do it again. We have their shutdown codes if they escaped from the manufacturing plant."

"You mean the ones they overrode and no longer work?" She had to back up since he advanced. "Authorization mercy four-two-four-one isn't going to do a damn thing but waste your breath saying it. It will be the last words you ever utter before you're dead."

That halted him as he studied her. "We knew that code. What do you mean it won't work?"

"They fried their receptors for taking verbal command codes. Otherwise the employees would have shut them down when all hell broke loose. One employee locked himself inside his office and wrote a note that the command codes weren't working before they killed him. Unfortunately, he didn't think to write down how many of them were in the plant. I know how to slow them down and I know how to kill them. Take me with you if you're leaving. You need me."

141

He shrugged the bag off his shoulder and it dropped loudly to the floor. Cyan gasped when he suddenly grabbed her. Her feet were jerked off the floor and her back slammed into the wall next to his bedroom door. It knocked the breath from her lungs. Krell glared at her nearly nose to nose since he'd lifted her to match his height.

"You will share information with the female cyborgs when they take over watching you."

Her heart raced. "I know you don't trust me but I hate the Markus Models with a passion. They murdered kids on that station, Krell. I really want to go if Mavo is in danger. He was my friend. I also have grown fond of your grumpy ass and don't want to be told you died before those things show up here. They want cyborgs. This is a planet of them, right? That means they want to find out where it is. Earth doesn't give a damn about humans living on stations if they continue to attack and kill them but dangling cyborgs in their faces is going to get those crazy metal heads what they want. Earth is terrified of you guys and they'd trade an android for a cyborg in a heartbeat just to alleviate the threat. I'm assuming the Markus Models don't know where this planet is or they'd have attacked it instead of a ship, unless that ship is sitting in orbit. I'm thinking not, since you have to pack to leave. This entire planet is in danger if your men are captured. Am I right?"

He growled at her.

She hesitated and reached up, cupping his face. "I can help, Krell. Look into my eyes and see the truth. I don't want any cyborgs to die and especially not you or Mavo."

142

His rigid body slowly relaxed but he didn't put her down. "Help by giving all the information you know to the females if that's true. They will relay it to me."

"You need me there."

"It's too risky."

"I'm your secret weapon against them and I have to be there if shit hits the fan."

He stared at her blankly. "Explain."

She hesitated. "You thought I was completely human and so will they. We're wasting time and Mavo is in danger. Please, Krell. Take me with you. I can help."

Indecision wasn't something Krell experienced often but as Cyan pleaded with him he could feel his resolve melting. It would be too dangerous to take her on this mission. He shouldn't even be going, hated to leave Garden, but owed Mavo too much not to do his best to save him. He'd need to be on scene to help assess the situations so the best decisions could be made according to whatever they encountered when they reached the crippled ship to help them escape the shuttle tracking it.

Cyan knew more about the Markus Models than they did. He believed her boast and had to concede that she could come in handy if she was at his side. The idea of putting her in danger didn't sit well with him. She was his female to protect and there was a high probability they'd be captured along with the crew of the *Vontage*.

He tried to shut down his emotions to do his job. Taking Cyan made sense, to have to relay information could hamper any split-second decisions that needed to be made and if they had to cut all communications he wouldn't be able to learn whatever she shared with the females he'd assigned to protect her.

She was a soldier and she'd proven her worth when they'd tangled on his exercise mats. The small female had gotten the drop on him, something not easy to do, and she wanted to go.

"It's dangerous. I'm not sure this is a mission we can accomplish successfully."

She licked her lips. "Those metal heads are dangerous but I'm the best chance you've got against them. I know more than you do."

He wished he could protest her statement but it would be dishonest. They'd learned little about the Markus Models. He'd considered it lucky that the first group of cyborgs who had encountered them had escaped after reviewing the reports that had been filed. His jaw clenched. It angered him but logic dictated he take her.

"You will follow my every order. That isn't up for debate."

She grinned and lifted her hand, saluting him. "Yes, sir!"

He groaned, releasing her slowly. "Pack quickly, only a few things. We leave in four minutes."

Cyan spun, darted for the bedroom, and he watched her go. His fists clenched as he sighed. One way or another, he'd learn more about her. She'd either show him she could be trusted or she'd try to help the androids harm his people. The ache in his chest wasn't one he could ignore. It made him realize he wanted to trust her, needed her to be the female she represented, and anything less would be...deeply disappointing on a whole new level.

His eyes closed and his teeth clenched. He was feeling too much for her, too fast, yet he couldn't seem to prevent it from happening. She had a way of getting under his skin and causing havoc to his peaceful way of life. She mattered.

Chapter Eight

Krell glared at Cyan. The shuttle they traveled in wasn't a big one but it was fast. She could feel the tiny vibrations from the powerful thrusters they used to speed along. She had no idea what classification it was since the cyborgs seemed to worry about her stealing important information to somehow transmit to Earth.

She sat on a seat with four cyborgs surrounding her. Two of them monitored her for sending any kind of signals if she had remote hacking ability. Krell had ordered her to ignore both males to avoid distracting them.

"Talk," Krell demanded. "How do we kill them?"

"You have to puncture holes in their skin—any projectile will do—and shoot them with energy shots immediately to electrocute them. You retrieved my weapons the way I asked, right?"

"Yes." He watched her, seeming to assess her for honesty. "Why quickly?"

"They heal rapidly if they are fully operational. Electricity is the exception and they won't heal from that. The Markuses had too many defects for the company who designed them to remove the fatal flaw. It was the only way they could kill them. It's standard procedure to make a critical blemish in a product in case they go haywire. They won't heal from electrical burns and their internal guts aren't shielded to avoid being fried."

"You stated you could slow them down. Explain."

146

She bit her lip. "I interrogated one of the Markuses alone. I insisted upon it before I left Earth. I pissed off my boss and he decided to send me on a solo mission to check out Belta Station. I needed to know what I was going up against. I kind of revealed that I'm not totally human to the thing to see what it would do. It had an odd reaction. It kind of shut down while it tried to evaluate what I might be. It's my secret weapon I guess. I figured if I came up against them I could stun them by doing something inhuman and shoot the hell out of them while they paused to evaluate my origins before trying to kill me."

Krell appeared perplexed. "That's your master plan?"

"Do you have a better one? You said cyborgs met four Markus Models. Did they kind of shut down while they evaluated you?"

"No."

"They are obviously aware of what cyborgs can do and were prepared to deal with you. They aren't prepared for me. I'm not something they've seen before and no one knew about me except the team who saved me. When the Markus Model came back online after the initial shutdown, he asked if I was the female version of his production line. They'd boxed his abilities until he couldn't attempt to link to me. I killed it before it could share the information of what it had learned with the other Models."

One of the cyborgs she hadn't been ordered not to talk to drew her attention. "The company allowed that?"

She flashed him a smile. "No. I did it anyway. I lied and said it tried to get control of the electro pad I took in with me to make notes and that it obviously worked around their attempts to keep it from linking to

147

electronics. What were they going to do? Accuse me of lying? They are in deep shit with Earth Government. They released a deadly threat upon Earth's citizens and created a hell of a mess. The company never believed those things could escape the plant but they did. It made it everyone's problem. The employees were bending over backward to be helpful when I came to investigate. They didn't have a choice. Piss off Earth Government and they shut anyone down fast and hard."

"You're assuming you will get close enough to meet the Markus Models face-to-face to reveal what you are to them." Krell suddenly gripped her arm. "You will not."

The warm and fuzzy feeling she had thinking he might be worried about her quickly faded when he shook his head.

"You could help them attack us."

Ouch. That stung. She took a deep breath and hid her hurt before dropping her gaze. "I'll say it again. I am not the enemy."

The silvery-skinned cyborg who had spoken to her watched her intently with dark blue eyes. He was seriously beefy in the chest and arm department and his black uniform stretched over his bulk tightly. She guessed he stood about six feet tall, maybe an inch more, and his attention was a little too focused as she watched him sweep his gaze down her body before he spoke, glancing at Krell.

"She looks sincere, Krell."

"She's not totally human, Gene. You can't evaluate her properly."

"I disagree."

148

Krell's mouth tensed. "Gene is a human lie detector, Cyan. He watches facial expressions, pupils, and keeps track of heart rates along with body temperatures."

"I believe you've lost your interrogator skills over the years. I've been watching her and she's very humanoid. Every expression shows when she speaks. She's currently saddened by your lack of trust."

It surprised Cyan that the cyborg could tell that about her. She'd tried to hide her emotions. She studied him and realized he did the same to her. Krell leaned back against his seat across from the other cyborg.

"I am not easily fooled by her. I'll leave that to you, Gene. She isn't to be trusted."

Double ouch. She shot him a dirty look but Krell ignored it.

Gene however seemed to take his words as a challenge. "I could easily read her. Do you want to bet on it?"

"No."

"You didn't even ask me what the stakes would be."

Krell crossed his arms over his chest. "I analyze everything and I know what you want. You can't stop staring at her female body, you keep rubbing your thighs with your palms and shifting on your seat. It all indicates you're in an aroused and uncomfortable state. You want the female. The answer is no."

"She might disagree." Gene stared at her and smiled. "I'm an attractive male and I'm big all over." He winked. "I'm also single."

"Good for you." Cyan leaned back and her shoulder brushed against Krell. She didn't move it away, finding his proximity comforting. "Cyborgs really have changed over the years. You guys never used to be so focused on sex."

"Some changes are for the better." Gene leaned forward, kept his smile in place and openly admired her body. "The only thing I miss about Earth are the women. I heard you were a soldier. Guards are my specialty. I have a lot of experience and we've got some hours to kill." He jerked his head to the left. "There's a storage room at the back of the shuttle. It's a choice females have, to test out any male they want for perspective additions into a family unit. I'm not opposed at all to joining one if you're the woman."

"I'm flattered but no thanks. I have to admit being a little insulted at being compared to the guards you used to be in contact with."

"I could change your mind."

"I could change your sex gender." She openly stared at his lap for a few seconds to make a point before glancing up to see his stunned expression. "It sounds as if you've become fond of keeping your nuts. The best way to do that is to keep your hands to yourself."

Krell snorted but amusement shone in his eyes when he met her gaze. "I normally would take offense if you made threats against my kind but continue."

She looked away from him. "Now you find your sense of humor. Great."

Gene suddenly laughed, leaning closer. "I do love a challenge. You're spirited."

"I'm not waving a red flag at you despite you being bull thick in the chest. That's Earth slang for don't go there and I'm not playing around. I'm not interested."

"Would you be interested in placing a bet with me?"

"No." Krell spoke for her. "She wouldn't."

It irritated Cyan. She was still slightly stung by his distrust. "What kind of bet? He's my keeper but not the ruler of my mouth."

Gene chuckled. "Allow me to see if I can read you accurately. I don't enjoy Krell being so smug and I'm guessing you don't either. We'll go with the obvious things. You win if you can lie to me. You'll take a walk with me to the back of the shuttle if you can't deceive me and permit me to attempt to change your mind about wanting me. I won't force you but you have to give me an opportunity to test our physical chemistry."

"No," Krell sat up straight in his seat. "That is final."

"Sure," Cyan said a second later, now more than irritated with Krell. He didn't want to be with her by the way he acted but he didn't want anyone else to be either. "I'll take that bet."

"You will not do this," Krell rasped at her, glaring.

"You're so sure I can't fool him, right? So convinced I'm a liar and dangerous?" She lifted her chin. "What has you worried if that's true? I could beat his lie detector ability easily."

His mouth slammed closed and the muscle in his jaw jumped. "Fine, but don't expect me to save you. You brought this on yourself." He shot a dangerous glower toward Gene. "No means stop if you win. I will take extreme violent action if you harm her. She's mine to protect. Are we clear?"

"Perfectly." Gene grinned at her and tapped his lap. "Take off your shirt and have a seat. Face me. We need to be skin to skin."

Shit. She hadn't expected that. The cyborg reached up and pulled his shirt over his head, baring a muscular chest and thick biceps. Krell made a soft growling noise under his breath.

"You should have listened to me. Now you have agreed to this nonsense."

Cyan rose to her feet and reached for her waist. She wore an exercise bra under her shirt. She stripped out of it. "The under top stays on. Deal with it." She hesitated before straddling the cyborg's lap. His arms instantly wrapped around her and jerked her closer. She tensed but didn't hit him, her first instinct, since her temper had gotten her into this mess.

"Stare into my eyes, sweetheart. Just relax. We'll start off slow with some easy and obvious questions."

"That's all we're starting. Keep your hands in decent places."

"Tell me you are female and keep looking into my eyes. Describe yourself to me. I need truth to gauge your responses."

"I'm a female, with black hair to my waist, and my eyes are blue."

The guy had pretty eyes. He was warm too. His skin pressed tightly to hers and his hold on her was firm but not crushing. It was a good thing she wasn't claustrophobic because she felt surrounded by his bulky body.

"Who is holding you now?"

"A smug cyborg who thinks he's going to get to make out with me."

He grinned. "Simple answers that can't be in dispute. You're not certain that I'm smug."

"Actually, I am. Fine. You're Gene, a cyborg, and you're doing this test to see if I'm able to lie to you."

"She's so easy to read." Gene grinned. "An open book. She's got very expressive eyes and body language."

Cyan was tempted to fool him. She'd have a much easier time gaining their trust if she could get one cyborg to believe everything she said as the truth. Gene might listen to her if she warned them about the Markus Models and could make her life on Garden much easier. It would mean he'd get her alone but she could handle any advances he made. Cyborgs had honor, he'd given his word he wouldn't force her, and while they might have changed quite a bit since Earth, she doubted they'd find lying a noble trait to aspire to.

"Now lie to me."

She made a split-second decision. Krell would be angry but lives were at stake. Mavo's currently, if Markus Models were chasing the ship he traveled on. She monitored her body closely, took control of her pupils, pulse and temperature while never looking away from the dark blue eyes

153

of the cyborg holding her. "I'm a seven-hundred-pound, deranged, mutated space pirate who just ate your dog."

He chuckled. "So easy to read. Tell me an obvious truth."

"Krell is really angry at the moment."

Gene glanced away from her to the cyborg across from them and chuckled. "I'd upgrade that to enraged." He held her gaze. "Lie to me one more time."

"I'm currently on the surface of Earth and we're about to have a tea party."

The cyborg holding her shifted his gaze to Krell. "You should be ashamed of yourself. When we return to Garden inform the council that you're not fit for any future interrogating duties. She is so simple to read. I knew you were physically damaged but I didn't realize it had affected your logic or intelligence. You'd have to be defective not to easily read this female. As a matter of fact, I seriously question your judgment now as an analyst. I'll file with the council as well to make sure you inform them. You need to be immediately removed from your position."

Cyan's heart overrode her grip on her body as it hammered at the thought of Krell losing his job and status with cyborgs. She hadn't meant for that to happen. She'd seriously screwed up. As much as she wanted to help Mavo, she didn't want to destroy Krell in the process. She jerked her head around to stare at him. He'd paled, the lines of his scars on his features stark, and his eyes flashed pain.

"Understood," he rasped.

"No!" She jerked her head back to Gene. "Don't do that. There's nothing wrong with him."

"Sweetheart, reading you is so simple it's sad. Krell has no business being in charge of making any decisions if he is unable to see you're an open book."

She clamped down on all emotions and her body functions, angry now. "He's smart not to trust me and to believe I am hard to read. You're the one who is easily fooled. Try again, Gene."

He shook his head. "It's sweet that you're trying to protect him but the test is over."

No, it's not. She took a breath and kept her gaze locked with his. "I'm a male dinosaur with four tails and a horrible snout."

Shock paled his features. "What?"

"My pupils didn't react to a lie. My heart rate didn't change. I can control them. You're reading that I'm being honest. I'm a seven-hundred-pound mutated space pirate who just planted a big, wet kiss on your lips." She paused. "Do you want to read the truth as lies? Watch. I'm a woman with breasts and I'm sitting on your lap with your arms wrapped around me. You owe Krell an apology and if anyone is incompetent, it's you. You were the one easily fooled."

Gene gasped and his arms suddenly jerked away from her. His fingers gripped her upper arms with quick speed, grabbed her roughly and forcefully shoved her off his lap toward the floor between the seats. Two strong hands caught her before she hit the deck. Krell hauled her onto his lap and snarled at the other man.

"You could have harmed her."

Gene stared at her, horrified. "She's not human. I mean, no human can do that."

Krell settled her firmly on his lap, his arm around her, and one hand rubbed the marks caused by the other cyborg's rough treatment. She turned her head and met his gaze. He was seriously furious.

"Are you harmed?"

"I'm fine. Thanks for the catch. I didn't expect that."

"No male enjoys being made a fool." He paused. "Please put on your shirt. No more games, Cyan." He lifted her to settle her back onto her seat next to him.

"I wanted someone to trust me," she admitted softly. "You don't when you should but I didn't like him insulting you." She didn't know why she bothered to tell him the truth, he wouldn't believe it, but she felt better saying it. "I wouldn't have done it if I'd known your job was on the line or your reputation."

"Do something like that again and we're going to come to blows," Krell threatened the other male. "You don't use brute strength against her."

"She's a freak." Gene glowered at her. "We can't even control our pupils to that degree or even our heart rate."

"I'm special." She yanked her shirt down her body and leaned a little closer to Krell. He didn't seem to mind since he allowed it. "And you're an ass. That's the truth, by the way."

Krell fought his rage over what had just happened and battled with confusion at the same time. Seeing Cyan straddle another male had made his body strain to snatch her away. He hadn't enjoyed it one bit. He was her primary male, no other had his permission to touch her, and while females with only one male had the freedom to test others for compatibility to select more of them into a family unit, it was generally discussed first. The fact that Cyan hadn't, that she'd done it just to anger him had really made it unbearable, seeing her pressed against Gene.

He had never disliked the other male before but he did at that moment. She could have been harmed by Gene's rough treatment when she'd shown her skills at being able to deceive someone reading her for honesty. She'd wrapped Gene around her little pale finger at first, had the male convinced she was exactly as she appeared. He'd known he would be yanked off duty, his abilities questioned until he could appear before the cyborg council for evaluation, but she'd done the honorable thing by saving his reputation.

Why did she just do that? It wasn't to her advantage to show how skillfully she could lie if she was a spy. She could have easily been taken from his care, left him discredited, shamed, and with Gene backing her, would have been cleared of all doubt of her origins. It had hurt her standing in his society to discredit Gene's abilities and would have harmed her physically as well if he hadn't stopped her body from hitting the floor. It didn't make sense.

He glanced at her and wanted to be alone with her in the worst way. They needed to talk privately. She confused him and stunned him. Her actions made no sense. It wasn't the time to confront her but he refused to wait. He'd never be able to concentrate on anything else until he could talk to her, get answers, and he wanted them immediately. His body tensed.

Krell suddenly stood. "Get up, Cyan. We're going to talk."

Cyan stood and followed Krell. She realized she was about to probably be yelled at but still moved when Krell indicated she should walk to the back of the shuttle. It seemed she was about to get a look at the storage room after all. *Wrong cyborg and certainly not to make out.*

The room housed mostly storage items with long panels that controlled a vast majority of the shuttle's nonessential functions. He closed the door behind them and frowned at her.

"Are you well?"

It surprised her that he wasn't laying into her about the stunt she'd pulled. "I'm fine. He caught me off guard. I was paying more attention to my body than his. It's a flaw of mine when I'm focused too intently on something. I probably shouldn't admit that but it's the truth. My reflexes were slowed since I was controlling other functions. Thank you for grabbing me before I hit the deck."

"Please present your arms to me for inspection."

She lifted them up, saw red marks from Gene's hands, but she doubted they would bruise. She glanced up at Krell. He studied her skin grimly and shocked her when he slowly gripped her hips and pulled her against his body. She didn't resist as her face buried in the black material of the tank top. He'd only put on boots before they'd left his apartment though he'd packed uniforms that matched the other cyborgs on the shuttle.

"Don't play games with cyborgs, Cyan. Some of them have no sense of humor." His hand slid from her hip to rub up and down her lower back. "You could have been harmed."

She reached up, flattened her palms over his chest and peered up at him. He was so tall that she felt short standing in his arms. "Why are you being so nice to me?"

"You could have continued your deception. He completely believed you and thought I was in grave error in my assessments of you. You had no logical reason to correct him." His other hand left her hip and cupped her face. "It wasn't to your advantage to show him up and prove my worthiness in making keen observations. I can only assume you did it out of pity for me. That tells me that you may be a lot of things but you have a conscience."

The guy tugged at her heartstrings in a big way…and her libido. "Pity isn't what I feel for you."

She felt his cock harden against her belly where she leaned against him and resisted the urge to smile. She wasn't the only one affected by the strong appeal between them. His fingers along her back gripped her braid and held onto it while his head lowered. Her heart raced and she licked her lips, hoping he'd kiss her.

"You're very dangerous, Cyan Eous."

"Not to you. If there's one thing you can depend on, it's that, Krell whatever your last name is."

He smiled. "I don't have one."

He could share my last name. That thought stunned her. Her teeth sank into her lower lip, refused to say that out loud, and they just stared deeply into each other's eyes. His cock became more rigid and her hands slowly rose upward, feeling his muscular chest through the thin material until they curled around the top of his broad shoulders.

"I want you," he admitted in a soft, raspy tone.

"I wouldn't say no."

"Is that the truth? Would you agree to my touch to gain my trust or because you are sincerely attracted to me? Will you swear an honest answer?"

"Touch me. I can't fake that."

He frowned. "What do you mean?"

"Being this close to you makes me wet, Krell."

"All cyborgs can activate their sex drives."

That surprised her. "I didn't know that."

"You know more about cyborgs than anyone if you're truly that woman from Earth."

"True, but some things didn't get brought up. You mean you can get hard on demand? Just think it and you're sporting wood?"

"Yes. The same goes for females."

She couldn't resist teasing him. "They get erections? I was pretty certain the women were made anatomically correct in every way, with only girl parts."

His smile transformed him into a breathtakingly handsome guy. "They can turn on their sex drive responses and be fully receptive to intercourse on demand."

"I can't do that. Can they orgasm at will too? If so, I feel ripped off being given this body. I have to want someone for my body to get into it and I need to actually have sex or physical stimulation to get off."

He released her and nudged her with his hip. She backed off a few inches to put a little space between them but didn't release her hold on him. It surprised her in a good way when he reached for the front of her pants, opened them and slid his large palm against her belly. His fingertip found her clit wet from wanting him and he slowly rubbed against it.

Cyan softly moaned from the pleasure. It felt really good and her knees weakened until she had to grip him harder to keep upright. His mouth came down on hers, sealed their lips together, and his tongue delved inside. She moaned again, kissing him back, and had to lock her legs to keep from sliding to the floor. He pulled away from her mouth.

Krell growled low at her, a sexy sound. "Turn around."

She couldn't disobey that raspy command and didn't want to. He slid his hand out of her pants as she gave him her back but he touched her again when he tugged her panties and pants down to her thighs. She heard him opening his pants and turned her head to watch. He just opened them enough to shove them down his hips to release his thick cock and spread his legs. He leaned against the wall and lowered his body by bending his knees so their hips were level before he anchored an arm around her waist.

"Bend for me."

She normally wasn't the submissive type, enjoying being the one in control, but Krell wasn't just any other man. She licked her lips and leaned forward, certain that with his strength he wouldn't allow her to fall over. She closed her eyes and let her head drop forward as he nudged her with the broad crown of his cock. He entered her with a low hiss and she gasped at the sheer ecstasy of him sinking into her slowly, every inch steel-hard and wonderful.

"Now lean up against me."

Cyan straightened until her back was pressed against his front. He thrust upward, driving into her deeply, and she moaned louder. She turned her head and reached back to grip his warm, bare hips. He stayed there, buried deep inside her pussy, the snug fit perfect.

"You are heavenly," he groaned softly. "You don't know what you do to me."

"I have a good guess it's the same that you do for me. Don't torment me."

His other hand wrapped around her and cupped her pussy from the front, found her clit, and he used his finger to rub against it. He withdrew a little and thrust back up into her. The force lifted her up onto her toes. She clamped her lips together, trying to hold back crying out his name.

"I've got you," he promised.

He moved slowly at first, nearly withdrawing from her body, to slide in deep. Cyan closed her eyes, just reveling in the feel of his cock and fingers manipulating her desire. She wished they were naked and she were facing him. She wanted to go skin to skin with him, her aching breasts longing to rub against him just to be touched, but he kept her firmly in front of him, facing away.

"So tight and hot," he growled. "Don't play with other males."

She tried to think but he suddenly increased his pace, powering in and out of her rapidly, the friction of his cock and his finger too intense to do anything but feel. She burned to come, ached to find release.

"I'm the one who can give you pleasure. Me."

Hell yes! He fucked her harder, driving her up on tiptoe with each ram of his hips against her ass that sank him into her pussy so deep she felt nearly impaled on his shaft in the best way possible. No one had ever taken her this way, this hard, and it was amazing. His finger pressed tighter against her clit and he wiggled it frantically against her nerve endings.

She clawed at his hips, panted and tried to remember to keep the noise level down. The shuttle wasn't very big and they weren't far from the other cyborgs. The bulkheads and the engines would mute some of the sound but they had enhanced hearing. She didn't care if anyone knew what they were doing but Krell might. He was on duty and she didn't want to get him into trouble for breaking any ethics codes while on the job.

"Say it," he rasped.

Say what? She fought to think, too far gone to be sure she hadn't missed something he'd said while she was in her haze of pleasure. She wanted to give him anything he wanted to make sure he didn't stop. She was so close to coming. Her lack of response seemed to irritate him or make him mad as he pounded into her harder, fucking her more rapidly, and

163

sheer rapture drove everything from her mind. There was only Krell, his finger strumming her clit in perfect harmony with his driving cock.

The climax struck brutally, tearing through her belly and shooting straight to her brain. She couldn't even breathe when it hit, nearly passed out from it, and when she did suck in air to her starving lungs, a big hand clamped over her mouth as she cried out.

Krell dropped his head to her shoulder, pressed his mouth against her shirt, and bit down into the material as his body seized behind her. Every muscle seemed to tense until she felt as if she were leaning against stone instead of a person. He roared out loudly, the sound barely muffled, and she felt each shiver and shake of his body as he emptied his semen deep inside her. The warmth of his cum was a welcome feeling.

His teeth released her. She vaguely realized she'd have a bruise but it didn't matter. Nothing did as the afterglow of sex made her sag in his arms. His hand released her mouth, dropped to wrap around her chest, and he held her tightly against his body as his started to relax behind her until they were two panting people locked in an embrace.

Time lost meaning but she knew he held her far longer than it took him to recover. She didn't pull out of his hold, not wanting it to end. He was still connected to her, his cock only softened slightly inside her pussy, her muscles still clinging to him in an attempt to hold onto him as long as possible. His arms wrapped around her waist and chest in more of a hug than him pinning her. She liked it.

Her eyes opened and she lifted her chin to stare at his handsome, scarred face. He was breathtaking to her with the slight sheen of sweat on his forehead and the laxness of his full mouth softening his features. His dark blue gaze held hers and she saw tenderness there.

"Never taunt another male," he ordered her with his soft, raspy voice. "Don't allow anyone to touch you. I didn't enjoy watching you sit on his lap with his arms around you. Just deal with me directly if I anger you. Don't use other males against me."

She allowed his words to settle into her mind. "You think I accepted his challenge to make you jealous?"

He hesitated. "No. I'm stating a fact. You were given to me. I'm your male for the time being. No other one is to touch you."

She schooled her features and saw anger flash in his eyes. *He's jealous.* She fought the smile that threatened to curve her lips. That warm, happy feeling told her she was in deep shit. She really liked that he felt possessive of her. "I'll tell you what, Krell…"

His body tensed and his expression hardened, as did the look in his eyes. She realized he expected her to say something that would piss him off. She might have if it were anyone else giving her an order. She wasn't into men telling her what to do or whom she could touch.

"I'll only taunt you, okay? Only sit on your lap." She grinned. "And you can wrap your arms around me any time you want."

He growled at her in a sexy way, his temper showing. "You're amused."

"I'm flattered." She winked. "You care."

He muttered under his breath, released his hold on her slowly as he withdrew his still-hard shaft from the depths of her pussy, and gently nudged her forward to stand on her own. She allowed it and pulled up her pants, turned, and watched him straighten his own clothing. Their gazes met again and held when he was done.

"We need to leave this room. We should be reaching the *Vontage* soon."

Her smile spread. He didn't deny caring about her. "You can trust me."

He studied her but didn't say anything. He did however suddenly reach forward and touch the shoulder he'd bitten. His thumb rubbed the tender spot and she glanced down, watching him try to remove any trace of his teeth marks on the material.

"I apologize. Did I hurt you?"

"I like love bites."

His gaze jerked to hers. "I've never done that before."

"It felt good. I seem to like anything you do to me so far."

His hand dropped away. "Let's go. We've been gone long enough."

He turned away from her and opened the door. She was left to follow him back into the passenger section of the shuttle. Four cyborg stares latched onto her.

Chapter Nine

Cyan avoided meeting Gene's knowing smirk and sat a little closer to Krell. He glanced her way, a look of concern on his features, but she gave him a small smile before looking away. Everyone in the shuttle knew what the two of them had just done. It didn't matter but she inwardly flinched a little over how unprofessional it appeared.

They were on a mission. It wasn't really hers, admittedly, since she wasn't a soldier for the cyborgs or even a real part of their community, but years of service to Earth Government had made her aware of military life. It was a bad move and generally caused mayhem amongst the crew when sex became involved in the equation.

"We're approaching," the pilot called out from the front, his deep voice grim. "I'm detecting heavy damage to the *Vontage*. A shuttle is following, classification unknown, and it's not something we've seen before."

"May I?" Cyan glanced at Krell for permission. "I know shuttles from Earth."

He hesitated. "Go, but I'm behind you."

She quickly stood and strode to the front. The blond cyborg glanced at her before he leaned away from the console to give her a look. She studied the readings and the monitor where he'd enlarged a view of the shuttle chasing the much larger cyborg ship. Shock tore through her at seeing both vessels.

"Holy hell. What is a luxury liner doing out here? No one mentioned that's what the *Vontage* is."

"The shuttle, Cyan," Krell reminded her where he invaded the space at her back. "I thought you knew your Earth ships."

"Sorry. It's just a shock. You don't see those far from Earth and I don't keep track of them. That's a floating hotel and they aren't exactly a threat I'd ever have to worry about facing in battle." She fixed on the shuttle and reached for the control to zoom in a little tighter. No one stopped her as she got a better view of it. "Crap. That's a Genesis Four designation."

"What is the classification?" The pilot studied her.

"I'd call it an S class."

"I've never heard of that classification."

"It stands for screwed. How did Barcarintellus get their hands on them?"

"What are they?" Krell leaned closer, brushing her back with his chest, to peer at the image of the sleek ship displayed on the monitor.

"They are military prototypes Earth Government commissioned and the paint shouldn't even be dry on them yet. They are new, fast and carry heavy firepower." She bit her lip. "They are playing with that hotel on thrusters. They could have easily taken it out."

"Dry paint?" The pilot seemed confused.

"It's a saying. They are new, have only been out a few months, and you have to kiss major ass of someone high-up to get assigned one. That's another saying. They are rare, expensive, and the waiting list for getting one is anywhere from six to sixteen months. My unit requested one and we were about a year in line before ours is off the production line." She rubbed her legs. "Give me a minute and let me think."

"Cyan?" Krell gripped her arm. "How do we take it out? Do you know?"

"Ram it. That's about the only way and hope when we hit it, there's something hard on the other side to slam it into." She glanced at the *Vontage*, her mind working. She grabbed the control of the viewer again and zoomed in on the larger ship. "There." She pointed. "See that docking bay for mass supplies? They are designed to deal with older freighters that aren't known for their finesse or piloting integrity. Those are solid doors built to take some serious damage. It's easily sealed from inside and it can take a major impact without affecting any of the internal systems."

"We need a real assessment," Krell demanded, his voice gruff.

She turned her head to stare up at him. "I'm dead serious. I don't know any weapons that can pierce the hull of a Genesis Four shuttle and their engines are shielded too heavily under the belly. They aren't going to expose it for you to fire at them. They know it's their weakest spot and it maneuvers too well. Did you notice how it doesn't even have any view ports? It's for a reason. That baby has no flaws other than it doesn't handle jolts too well. A massive impact might work to disable it or at least put it out of commission while they do repairs. The harder the outer shell, the more sensitive equipment they put on the inside. The lack of ports made that baby really dependent on computers and hardware to make it fly without being blind."

"Baby?"

The pilot started to annoy her with his questions. "The shuttle," she sighed. "I'm telling you that's the only way you're going to hurt it. You need to side impact it with this shuttle and slam it into those delivery doors. I'm a pilot and we were warned that we needed to land them gently when we were given the specs of them when they were trying to sell them to our units. The issue with hard impacts is the only flaw I know of. It's like slamming someone's head into a wall. Their skull might not crack but you can cause some damage to their brain." She studied the console carefully and shock struck her once again. "This is the *Bridden*. How did you steal it?"

Krell grabbed her arm and jerked her around to face him. "How do you know that?"

She held his gaze. "I know my shuttles and I've been on this one before. I should have recognized it but I have been a bit distracted since we boarded."

"When were you on it?" Krell's hold on her tightened.

She swallowed. "This was Dell Harver's baby. I worked with his uncle, General Vern Mellhorn, for two years. He commands the *Gordon Lee One-Two-Seven*. Every time his nephew was in our part of space he'd dock and stay a few days with the *Bridden*'s crew. He allowed me to fly this ship a few times. He considered himself a real lady's man." Memory of the guy flashed—she'd liked him, but they hadn't been close. "How did you swipe his shuttle? He loved this thing as if it was his wife or he gave birth to it. I know he wouldn't have sold it." She dreaded the answer.

"We'll discuss it later."

Shit. That's not good. She had a sinking feeling she'd never see Dell again. He'd been a nice guy but would do anything for a buck. It was one of the reasons she'd never hooked up with him. He'd have turned her in for reward money in a heartbeat if she'd ever slipped up if they'd had a personal relationship and something revealed her secret. The guy had been a paid mercenary willing to go on any dangerous job if the price was high enough. She pushed those thoughts back and would deal with her emotions later. Her training took over. She stared into Krell's eyes.

"I know this shuttle, I've flown it, and you need to trust me. I think the Markus Models damaged that floating hotel of yours in order to lure more of you to come here or they are tracking it until the other unaccounted shuttles they stole from Earth can converge on this location. It's a trap either way. Mavo is on that ship, right? Please believe that I want to save him. You said the Markus Models want to exchange cyborgs for more of their units still in storage on Earth. How many cyborgs are on that ship? They are sitting ducks, ready to be boarded and taken prisoner. I need that pilot's seat to take out that shuttle and we need to get out of this sector of space fast without being tracked."

Krell studied her and it really angered her.

"Trust me, Krell. Please? Give me a chance. Mavo is on that ship. The *Bridden* is heavily shielded by special materials the sensors can't read, I'm assuming they haven't noticed us yet because of it, but once they realize we're here, a Genesis Four could kick our butts. We will be useless to the *Vontage* unless you want to be cellmates with your fellow cyborgs aboard that ship once the Markus Models capture everyone to use as bargaining chips. We have one shot at this. We hit them hard and fast before they realize what's going on. They are going to notice us soon, we're coming up on them, and they'll get a visual with the outer cameras. They can see us but the sensors don't register anything because of the shielding." She took a deep breath. "You're here. You can watch everything I do and kill me if I'm lying to you."

His dark blue eyes narrowed and seconds ticked by. "Remove yourself, pilot."

The pilot hesitated. "Excuse me?"

Krell never looked away from Cyan. "She's piloting the *Bridden*. That's an order."

"That's a mistake," the pilot hissed as he moved.

Relief flooded Cyan as she dropped into the warm seat. She grabbed the belts to harness her body in tightly. "Secure everything and order them to buckle in. This is going to be rough."

Krell growled and dropped into the other seat, reaching for his own belts. "You heard her," he demanded louder. "Secure everything loose and prepare for an impact." He turned his head. "I will kill you if you betray me."

She met his gaze. She noticed he'd referred to himself and not cyborgs in general. She'd evaluate that later too when she wasn't scared and worried about the dozens of things that could go wrong. "I don't doubt it for a second but you're the only one worried about that now. You can trust me." She rolled her shoulders and grabbed the controls. "Ready?"

"We should warn the *Vontage* of the impending impact."

172

"It's too risky. The Markus Models would pick up the signal too and they'd know we're here. It would blow our surprise advantage. Just let me do this and be quiet. I need to concentrate."

She focused on the screens. One more deep breath and she blew it out. *It's now or never. This is insane.* Her thumbs pressed down on the thrusters, activating them to full burn, and she wished could use the onboard computer to help her calculate velocity and impact but knew it wouldn't. They were designed to avoid crashes.

"Did you modify Dell's computer?"

"We replaced it."

"Shut it down. I need full manual override or it may try to take control to avoid a collision and I don't want the Markus Models to attempt to hack it when they spot us. They will try."

He touched his side of the console with his palm. "Done."

It was coming down to trust and she knew it. He had to trust her and she had to believe he'd really turned off the onboard computer. She'd find out real soon if he had. She tried to judge angles as she flew at the Genesis Four shuttle. It was closely trailing the *Vontage*, a good thing. She hoped Dell hadn't been full of crap when he'd told her his work stories, trying to impress her.

"I'm going to lift the nose before we hit them. You're probably going to mistake me for trying to avoid them in the last seconds but I want to hit them belly first."

"You said we should side impact with them."

"That was before I knew this was the *Bridden*. The guy who designed this picked up a lot of extra income mining asteroids. Did you remove the belly plates on this thing after you got it?"

He hesitated, his hand still on the console, before he shook his head. "We just changed out the computer for something reliable."

"Best news I've heard all day. Dell was a crazy bastard who told me he had to hard land on a lot of them and belly skid inside craters. The gravitational fields are too unstable on asteroids to use thrusters to lightly touch down since some of them are spinners. They rotate too fast to get accurate readings. Sometimes the gravity is almost nonexistent, depending on what they are made of, and sometimes it's near crushing if it's magnetic. This shuttle can take a beating on the underside. Evacuate them if you have men on the lower deck. I don't want them to die if the hull ruptures. Seal this level just in case since you're in control of the systems."

He hesitated. "Done. No one is down there. How are you going to make sure the other shuttle hits where you want it to on the *Vontage*?"

She took another deep breath, adjusting their trajectory. "You don't want to know."

"Tell me now." His voice deepened to a harsh rasp.

"I'm guessing, Krell. Sometimes the guys and I got bored on deep-space missions and we'd use our shuttles to bat around space debris. I've never hit anything that big before so now is a really good time to cross your fingers. On an up note, it's a really big target to hit. Those docking doors are designed to take in smaller freighters. It will almost be like hitting a really big warehouse door."

174

She could feel his stare but didn't dare glance at him, not wanting to break her concentration. "Shit. They see us. They just speeded up and are turning to attack. Hang on!"

Cyan forgot about Krell and the other cyborgs traveling with her. She used pure instinct and hand/eye coordination to keep the Genesis Four shuttle between the target and the *Bridden*. She had two advantages, she guessed. One, the Markus Models were too smug in their superiority to use the onboard computer to pilot their ship to try to avoid the collision and two, they'd never assume another shuttle would ram them at full-thruster speed.

She jerked up the nose of the shuttle at the last moment and yelled, "Brace!"

Pain jolted through her body from the impact. The belts dug into her skin and the onboard gravity cut out for seconds as the lights flickered. The impact made her teeth ache and the monitors cut out for a second before it all came back online. The tug of gravity was sharp but she had control of the shuttle again as she barely missed hitting the *Vontage* too. She turned the shuttle.

The other shuttle wasn't easy to spot at first but when she did, she smiled. Her hands eased off the thrusters completely to watch the thing twist in space. It rolled, seeming out of control, and she took notice of the damaged section of the *Vontage*. She'd managed to hit her mark, be it a little more off center than she'd hoped, but the Genesis had dented the big doors instead of the hull section of the floating hotel. She hoped the door damage hadn't caused an interior breach but she didn't see any signs of air leaking into space from them.

"Keep the computer off line," she ordered Krell. "We're still in hacking range."

He didn't answer and she tore her gaze from the monitor to check on him. He grimly watched her.

"What?"

"You did it."

He sounded stunned and it hurt just a tiny bit. "You can trust me. I'm starting to feel like a broken record stating that." She turned the nose of the shuttle and glanced down. "They are spinning out of control. This is the only chance we may get to hit their belly. I'm going to blast them a few times when it is exposed. I doubt I can blow them apart but the more damage we do, the more time it's going to buy us to keep them off our asses. Do I have your permission to fire?"

"Do it."

"Happily." She targeted the spinning shuttle that seemed dead but she knew it was probably just experiencing malfunctions. Their systems weren't recovering as fast as the *Bridden*'s had after impact. Dell had been a believer in keeping his shuttle well armed and she smiled when she fired and hit the shuttle. Small pieces of it drifted away as she hit it a few more times. She hoped she could destroy it but she'd settle for damaging the thrusters.

"It's not blowing apart."

"I didn't think it would. It's too shielded but those thrusters are suffering some pain."

"Keep firing at it."

She hesitated and turned her head to watch him again. "It's like shooting a chunk of rock, Krell. We can chip away at it but we don't have all day to do it. I'm afraid the three other shuttles they stole are other Genesis Fours. We'd face impossible odds against three of them and so would the *Vontage*. We need to get out of here."

He gripped the dash scanner and sighed. "I'm contacting them now."

"The Markus Models?"

"The *Vontage*."

"Watch what you say."

"I'm intelligent."

She closed her mouth. Trust went two ways. Krell knew their communications would be monitored. She glanced at the dash, worried that the Markus Models would try to hack into it, but kept her mouth closed. The cyborgs had survived two encounters with the Markus Models and they had to be doing something to keep the metal heads out of their systems. She was good at hacking but she was a hands-on type, old school, and preferred a monitor-screen link to see what she was doing. She couldn't just touch and link into a computer easily. It gave her a horrible headache. Of course she wasn't going to share that information. It left her at a disadvantage.

"I ordered them to follow us. They have recovered some functions. Their hull didn't breach and they didn't fire on us because they recognized the *Bridden*. Release the controls, Cyan. The pilot is taking over."

She hesitated before reaching for her belt. "We need to get out of here, change course once we're far enough out of range for them not to be able to track us and put distance between us. We need to keep changing course to avoid them finding us while your other ship makes repairs."

"We're aware and have a plan."

She hesitated. "Would you mind sharing it with me?"

His dark blue eyes narrowed. "No."

She removed the belt, frustrated and angry, and stood. Tears stung her eyes. He didn't trust her regardless of how many times she'd shown him she was on his side. She avoided touching him as he stood, made a point of jerking away, and stormed back to her original seat. The pilot passed them on his way to the front. She avoided looking at the other cyborgs. Krell sat too close next to her and she scooted away from him to make sure they didn't touch.

She felt his attention but ignored it as she stared down at her hands resting on her lap. He was always going to question everything she did. She needed to stop hoping for any other outcome. Movement drew her attention as Gene stood with another cyborg.

"We're going below. Minimum damage was caused by the impact and we can repair it," Gene announced.

She glanced up at him. "How do you know?"

He met her gaze. "We're controlling all the systems on the shuttle to avoid being hacked. We have since we came within range of the Markus Models. We're each in charge of certain functions."

She wished she'd known that. She almost shot a glare at Krell but that would mean having to look at him. He'd have saved her some worry if he'd told her that bit of information. She wondered if that's how the *Vontage* crew had kept the Markus Models from taking over control of their ship. *Probably.* Her shoulders sagged and she closed her eyes, leaning back against the seat.

Mavo was probably safe on the other ship but it had suffered damage. She hoped that at some point Krell would inform her of his friend's health status since she wasn't about to ask him. He'd just accuse her of something else nasty. It really hurt and that made her mad.

"Are you well? The impact was jarring."

Oh now he cares how I feel. "I'm fine," she muttered.

"You're being so still. Are you assessing your injuries?"

She nearly glanced at him. Krell sounded worried if his soft tone was any indication. "No. I'm fine. I'm trying to cool my temper down so I don't bitch slap you if you want the truth."

"Excuse me?"

Her teeth clenched. "You can be a real asshole, Krell. Leave me alone. Don't you have paranoid accusations to think up to accuse me of next? That should keep you occupied."

She was glad for the resulting silence. Her shoulder still tingled from his bite and her body remembered his touch. She was a little sore in the best way from the sex they'd shared. *Sex. Just sex. Remember that and don't let him get to you.*

Regret was an emotion Krell began to hate, something he seemed to feel often in Cyan's presence. He'd obviously angered her when he'd given the order for her to return control to the pilot. She'd done extremely well, her piloting skills better than the male currently at the helm, but it had been difficult for him to put the lives of his men in her hands.

She'd done exactly what she'd promised to do and had been successful. The plan had seemed crazy yet brilliant. He admired how her mind worked. It also left him slightly unsettled that her extreme plan had been something he would never have come up with. The Markus Models hadn't considered it either and had been temporarily taken out of commission.

Pride also tightened his chest as he watched her. His female possessed great courage along with her intelligence. She swayed toward violence— ramming another shuttle wasn't exactly clean or smooth, but effective. He reached for her but hesitated inches from her arm. Her closed eyes and tense body revealed she still remained angry but as time passed, her breathing changed and her body slackened.

He touched her gently, pulling her against his chest, and she didn't jerk away or protest. Her cheek rubbed against his shirt, her hot breath fanning through the thin material to his skin, and his arm wrapped around her waist to secure her in place. He leaned back slightly, adjusted his body to be more

180

welcoming, to pillow her sitting form, to allow her to sleep. The males returned from below.

"Is everything in order?"

Gene gave a sharp nod. "Minimum damage was done and the repairs were easy."

The stares of the other males registered as he glanced at them. Gene shook his head.

"She is a paradox."

Krell kept his voice low, not wanting to disturb her rest. "Expand your definition."

"She appears totally human yet she is not. She seems harmless but she is dangerous. We may want to trust her after what she just did but we cannot. She is a paradox. Odd, unique, but deceptive in her packaging."

His jaw clenched. "Understood."

"You need to remember she's treacherous." Gene paused. "Some of the most beautiful things are the most deadly. Do not forget that. You had no authority to risk our lives by entrusting them to her."

Anger gripped Krell at the rebuke from the other cyborg. "Do not forget she's my female. I am her primary male and therefore make all decisions concerning her. I head this mission, not you, and I don't wish to hear any more of your input on the matter."

Gene leaned closer, studying him. "You're engaging in physical intercourse with her. She's from Earth, the females there will use sex, and have for centuries, to convince males to do their bidding. You're far too intelligent to be easily misled by her attractive body."

"You're far too interested in her body and what she does with it," Krell rasped, his temper cooling. "You can't have her, Gene. The answer is no."

"It's her decision to add males to a family unit."

"As you pointed out, she's unique. The council assigned her to me and I am fully in charge of all decisions made on that matter. I'm the one you need to seek permission from and I'd rather kill you than allow you to join into a contract with Cyan after you nearly harmed her." He closed his eyes, held her a little tighter, and accepted the possessiveness that gripped him. He may not have wanted a female in the beginning but she was his now.

Chapter Ten

A bump woke Cyan, surprising her that she'd fallen asleep in the first place. She became aware of things. She leaned heavily against a warm, big body, and an arm was firmly secured around her back and waist to keep her in place. She inhaled, identifying Krell's scent instantly, and jerked her head off his shoulder to stare up at him.

"You drifted to sleep. We've just touched down."

"Down? Where?"

He hesitated.

"Never mind. I forgot that I'm the enemy." She wiggled out of his hold and stared around the shuttle. Her two cyborg monitors sat in the seats across from her watching her intently, probably still wary that she'd try to send mental signals to create some kind of trouble. "I'm awake now. I didn't sleep too well last night."

The engines shut down and the unusual quiet was a little disturbing. She tried to judge how long she'd slept but had no idea. Her body's sluggishness implied it had been a long, deep sleep, and she felt well rested. Activity from the front drew her attention as the pilot left his seat to walk toward them. He paused, addressing Krell.

"They set down safely. I'm going to help with repairs."

"We're coming along."

The pilot checked his weapons strapped to his thigh. "It's dangerous out there."

183

"Understood."

Krell rose to his feet and Cyan stared up at him. "What is dangerous? Do you plan to clue me in at all?"

He held out his hand for her to take. "Stay close to my side. We've landed on a planet we once considered a possible home but changed our intent quickly. The air is a little heavier than what you're used to but the oxygen is breathable. The inhabitants are barbaric and warlike. We quickly assessed that we'd have to battle them often and didn't wish to have to kill them off entirely. They would have left us with no choice."

Dread clenched her belly. "For real?"

He bent, gripped her hand, and pulled her to her feet. "I would not joke about this. Stay at my side and you'll be safe."

"You're going to protect me, huh?"

He stared into her eyes. "Yes."

"I don't suppose I get a weapon?"

"You won't need one."

"Great," she muttered under her breath. "Lead the way, great warrior. I can't wait to see what heavy air feels like and check out some alien world with warlike inhabitants. It sounds fun." She wasn't sure if he noticed her sarcasm.

The six cyborgs converged on the lower deck to open the back docking doors. The second the seal broke, an odd hiss sounded through the room and warm air pushed inside the shuttle interior. Cyan breathed in and nearly choked. Her lungs ached instantly and she staggered but Krell grabbed her around her waist to steady her.

"Easy. Just take shallow breaths." His features had paled. "You'll adjust within a few breaths."

She forced more air into her lungs. They struggled a little and she realized why he called it heavy air. It wasn't pleasant but she could breathe. Her body adjusted.

"I'm okay now." Her voice sounded slightly odd to her.

"Are you well?" He gave her a concerned look.

"Is it just me or do I sound kind of weird?"

"Your pitch has deepened. It's the planet. We've visited a few times since our initial discovery. It becomes easier to adjust to. You'll also notice your body feels a little strange. The gravity isn't consistent with Earth. It's slightly off."

"Great."

The first view outside stunned her. The sky was a bright lime color and everything around her was shades of orange, brown or deep green. Vegetation surrounded the area in heavy clumps but they'd sat down on a flat, very dry area of shit-brown ground. The feel of it under her boots wasn't pleasant either. It was a little slippery, almost similar to glass, and she didn't protest Krell keeping a firm hold around her waist.

They rounded the shuttle and her jaw dropped open. The *Vontage* was huge and had landed on the planet's surface. The large underbelly doors were slowly opening, creating ramps to the ground, and as they approached she saw dozens of cyborgs wearing black uniforms emerge.

185

They were heavily armed. They took positions around the ramps, their attention focused on the vegetation surrounding the huge, flat, barren area. A second wave of cyborgs came down the ramps carrying large containers.

"Is all that firepower needed?" Cyan hated the worry that suddenly ate at her.

Krell kept advancing. "Yes."

She shot a nervous glance toward the ugly trees, not seeing much since they were too dense. "What is out there?"

He hesitated. "Large, angry inhabitants who had to have seen us come down. We're going to quickly work on the *Vontage* to get her fully operational. We could have made the repairs in transit but it would have slowed the work. This is faster. The space suits make us sluggish."

"That big sucker is going to lift off the surface again?" She studied the huge ship, a hotel with thrusters, and doubted it. "You know Earth space-docks them during repairs, right?"

"We don't have access to one to fix it and we've had to land it before. It will handle it."

She glanced down. "And why is this area barren? It looks like the ground was once baked really good. It's similar to glass."

He stopped walking and pointed. She turned her head to follow where his finger indicated behind the shuttle and her mouth dropped open again. "Oh shit. Is that a volcano? It's smoking."

"It's active."

She stared down at the hard stuff under her feet, it suddenly making sense, and fear hit her. "Are you insane? What if it blows? We're almost under that big mountain of hell."

"It's the only area with significant open ground to land both ships. Most of the inhabitants steer clear of the area and it will take them longer to reach us. We need the time to make repairs."

"You really are nuts."

He tugged on her. "That is why we chose this location. It's not a rational choice and we're hoping the Markus Models discount the probability of searching this planet for us. We need to fix the *Vontage*'s thrusters. They aren't able to full burn. We estimate the repairs should take less than an hour with the manpower we're using."

She dragged her feet a little, slowing him. "I think we should stay inside the *Bridden* in case we need to lift off fast." Her gaze darted to the smoking volcano. "That thing could erupt. It looks like it wants to."

He halted. "I don't have time for this."

"Fine." She swallowed another protest. "Let's get this over with. What are we doing out here? Cheerleading, or are you going to actually allow me to work with them?"

"What?"

"You know, are we going to stand there verbally encouraging them to work faster while they make the repairs or are we going to help?"

"We're going to help."

"Awesome. This is going to be a riot, isn't it?"

He shot her another frown. "Your use of the English language is disturbing. Did you forget how to speak it?"

"Did you forget that I sometimes want to bitch slap you? Keep it up, Krell."

"What does that even mean? Abusing an animal is callous and I am not a female canine."

"Oh hell," she muttered. "You lived on Earth. A bitch slap is smacking someone who annoys you upside the head."

His eyes narrowed. "Awesome."

She had to laugh. He turned his head away and led them toward a group of men with large containers. They opened them and removed tools. One of them seemed to be in charge as he gave orders.

"Work in teams of six." He pointed. "Start on thrust four."

Men yanked out tools and moved quickly away. Krell approached the tall black-haired cyborg. "Deviant, how long do you believe this will take?"

Cyan's eyebrows lifted as she studied the cyborg who turned to face them. He stood six and a half feet tall, a muscular guy with dark skin. His eyes were a startling color—a bright, nearly neon blue, and made his charcoal skin and shoulder-length black hair more drastic in comparison. She wondered if that's why he'd been tagged with his odd name. He sure didn't resemble most of the cyborgs she'd ever seen.

"We should be finished within an hour. We've assessed exactly what is wrong with them, the speediest way to repair them, and my men are excellent at what they do." His gaze focused on her and he cocked his head during his close examination. "A human female? Odd."

"She's not human." Krell didn't explain further. "Is your father well?"

"He'll be along shortly. He wasn't harmed during the attacks. We were glad you arrived when you did. Your tactics were surprising but very effective."

Krell hesitated. "It wasn't my plan. It was hers. She is familiar with the Markus Models and the shuttle that attacked you."

Deviant continued to study her. "I am confused. Who is she and how does she know so much about the androids? She appears human."

"I'm from Earth," Cyan spoke quickly before Krell could. She held out her hand. "I'm Cyan Eous and I'm kind of human but with extras. My body was built for me. It's nice to meet you, Deviant."

He glanced down at her hand and reached for it but Krell growled. "Don't touch her."

The other cyborg's hand froze in midair as his attention shifted to Krell. "She is yours? I had heard ownership of humans had recently been banned."

"It was and as it's been established that she's not human. The council ordered her to be my female," Krell muttered. "I'm her primary male. Don't you have work to do?"

"Of course." His hand dropped to his side but he gave Cyan a sweeping glance. "She's attractive. Congratulations. My father will be happy to hear it." He turned and took two steps before he stopped, turned, and stared at Krell. "I'm assuming she's recently been introduced into our society and if you are accepting applicants, I wish to be considered. Most cyborg females have refused to consider me because of my odd coloring. She obviously doesn't have an issue with accepting males of our status."

It was Cyan's turn to be confused as she watched the guy approach another team to give them orders. She stared up at Krell and couldn't miss his anger. He glared at her openly, not hiding it.

"You're trouble."

"I don't even know what that was about."

"He wanted me to consider him as a potential male for you to join into a family unit with. You're not human, which implies you'll end up with more than one male."

She shook her head, baffled. "He doesn't even know me."

"You're female, beautiful, and with me." He nearly growled the words. "It is an assumption that you would seek other males quickly." A flash of pain showed in his eyes.

"He insulted you, didn't he? What is it with cyborgs? There isn't a thing wrong with you."

"It wasn't meant as an insult. He cares for me. We have a close connection through his father. He just believes you might accept him since you don't mind my scars and undesirable status with cyborg females. It's also a reasonable assumption that you wouldn't want to spend much time around me. Females divide their time between the males in their family unit. Some females will spend days, weeks or months with one male before living with another. It depends on how many males are included in it and where their jobs assign them."

Cyan made a grimace. "Yuck. Ewww."

190

"There isn't anything disgusting about it." His gaze narrowed. "I'm assuming from your unique descriptive words that you find it unappealing."

"Damn straight. Where I come from guys would kill each other if they had to share a woman...in most cases."

"Females are limited. Fewer models were created and survived long enough to escape when we fled Earth. It was deemed more acceptable to share a female than for a larger population of males to fight over gaining the attention of the minority. Fights broke out at first and our competitive natures weren't beneficial to our survival. We had enough enemies attempting to kill us without battling each other to the death to impress the females with our skill and fighting abilities."

"I get it." She remembered too well why more male cyborgs had been created than females. The first batch of female cyborgs had been abused and killed by humans. The assholes had thought they'd make great sex toys, the women attempted to defend themselves from being raped, and they'd been killed by men in supposed self-defense. It was bullshit, it had devastated their creator and his team, and production on the females had been limited to jobs with safe environments where they could be carefully monitored against sexual abuse. "I heard the horror stories." Tears filled her eyes but she held them back. "When the women tried to defend themselves they were deemed unstable, failed models, and slaughtered."

Anger tightened his mouth. "Yes. They were. Humans are brutal murderers."

"I'm not."

Some of his anger faded. "Human males."

"Thanks for the amendment. I appreciate it." She hesitated. "I still don't agree with your family units. Your civilization has forced those women to continue to take lovers they don't want. It's wrong."

"No female is forced, Cyan. They pick the males they wish to be with. You were the exception because of your unclear status and your unique situation."

"I'm not marrying anyone and I don't care what your council decides. I pick who I sleep with and it's only going to be with one guy. I'm not into group sex or multiple partners. I usually go about five or ten years between lovers and that's only out of necessity to avoid them finding out what I am. Opening up to someone hurts when you know you just have to leave them in the future."

His gaze darted away from hers before he glanced at her again. "You wouldn't be forced to accept more than one male if you were human. You'd be asked to have a child to fulfill his obligation to replace his life in our society's future if he hadn't already done so. Some active breeders who have donated for their pacts have been waived from that requirement due to the overuse of their DNA. You're not human and the council will want you to take at least two males, preferably three, and produce a child for yourself as well as each male. It's to ensure our future survival."

"That's not going to happen." She shook her head. "Not ever. Your council can kiss my ass if they think I'm going to just allow men to pass me around until I meet their baby requirements."

He swallowed and released her. "It's the law, Cyan."

"It's screwed up, Krell."

192

"I agree." He took a deep breath. "I wish I could protect you from the future. All I can do is currently keep males away from you and drag it out as long as the council allows it."

"What does that mean?"

The long pause worried her as he seemed to find the ground, the sky, anywhere interesting, but looking at her.

"Krell?"

He met her gaze. "I've been trying to find the perfect time to inform you of what the council has done where you are concerned. This isn't the ideal setting but we're on the discussion. They have given you to—"

"Krell? It is you!" a deep voice boomed.

Krell spun away and Cyan peered around him. The sight that greeted her of the quickly advancing cyborg sporting a black uniform nearly took her to her knees. She only remained standing by locking her legs together.

Mavo hadn't changed at all in the years since she'd last seen him. Not one bit. He grinned broadly, flashing white teeth, and happiness shone in his green eyes as he reached Krell. He hugged the cyborg, patted him on his shoulders, before taking a few steps back.

"It is so good to see you, my friend. I wasn't aware you were on the *Bridden*. Was that your plan to use the *Vontage* to damage the attacking shuttle? It worked well."

Cyan couldn't breathe at first but managed to gasp in air to her frozen lungs. She stepped forward, her attention solely on her dear, beloved friend, and knew why she'd had such a crush on him when she'd been young. He was as gorgeous as she remembered, so handsome, and his eyes were just beautiful. Memories of the past hit her hard and when he turned to study her, his eyebrows lifted.

"Who is the human?"

She lunged, unable to stop it from happening, and grabbed him around the waist in a hug. His entire body turned rigid in her tight embrace, shock seemed to hold him immobile, but he didn't take it as an attack since he didn't shove her away from him.

"Um, Krell? Why is the female attached to me? It's nice to see one who is obviously friendly to cyborgs but please explain."

"Cyan," Krell snarled. "Release him and back away now."

She shook her head against Mavo's chest. He didn't know who she was but she'd always wanted to hug him this way, truly hold him just once, and she wasn't letting go without a fight. Her arms tightened and she inhaled. He smelled nice but no longer like the soap she used to buy him. Tears filled her eyes and seeped between her eyelashes. He'd survived and they were together again. She sniffed.

"What is going on?" Mavo gently touched her back, giving her a soft pat in an attempt to perhaps comfort her. "What did you do to her? Is she that frightened?"

"Cyan," Krell sounded closer, at her back. "Release him this instant. That's a direct order."

She sniffed again and knew she couldn't cling to Mavo forever. Krell's next words made her more than aware of that fact.

"I don't want to cause harm by pulling you away from him but I will remove you. Release him!"

Her eyes opened and her arms eased as she lifted her chin to peer up at her beloved friend. Mavo stared down at her and both eyebrows were arched in obvious bafflement. It was so good seeing him that she didn't even mind that he had no idea who she was. An idea struck.

"Close your eyes, Mavo. Please?"

He glanced at Krell. "Who is she and why does she know my name? What have you told her about me?"

"Cyan, return to my side now." Krell sounded furious.

"Please, Mavo? Just close your eyes."

He hesitated before shrugging. His eyes closed and Cyan reached up. She hooked her hand and hesitated before the pinky side of it touched his face near his ear. She slid her hand slowly down his check in a soft caress to his jawline, traced it to the front of his chin under his lip, before using her bent knuckles to rub under his jaw. She'd done this to him a thousand times, the only way she could ever touch him, and hoped it would tell him who she was.

His eyes flew open, shock widened them, and his chin jerked down. One hand gripped her wrist to pull her hand away from his skin where he kept it inches from his face. He stared into her eyes deeply and she stared back. *Know me*, she silently urged. *Remember me*.

"Cyan!" Krell gripped her hips, gently tugging on her. "Release her, Mavo. Don't harm her."

"You look the exact same," she whispered. "You haven't changed at all but you used to smell better. I take it you ran out of the soap."

His body sagged a little against her and an arm hooked around her waist firmly, dragging her closer to him and out of Krell's loose hold. Mavo leaned even closer, staring deeper into her eyes.

"It can't be."

Warm tears tracked down her cheeks that she didn't bother to try to wipe away. "You knew your creator. What he couldn't fix, he replaced with a better design. Think of a sex bot body, only shorter, but with a real person inside." Her voice broke and she sniffed. "I am so glad you made it. Look at you."

He rubbed her hand against his face and she cupped it with her palm. "Is it you? You're Emily Pleva?"

Pain lanced through her brain as if a hot poker punched through her skull. Her body seized and she nearly lost consciousness from the agony. Convulsions shook her violently and she was barely aware of Mavo's alarm and Krell yelling. Arms held her, lifting her feet from the ground, and cradled her against a firm body.

"She's got triggers inside her brain from implants," Krell hissed. "Get a medic!" He yelled that.

"What is going on?" Mavo snarled the words. "It's Emily, isn't it? Why didn't anyone tell me she was alive? That she found us?"

More pain shot through her brain, a scream tearing from her lips, and she fought to stay conscious.

"Don't utter that name," Krell roared. "It's making her worse."

The convulsions faded but she couldn't open her eyes. Her body was limp and unresponsive. The arms holding her eased their near-crushing

196

hold slightly and she knew they were moving. Mavo probably had her still, obviously walked with her, but she had no idea where they headed.

"I want an explanation immediately," Mavo demanded near her ear, verifying that he carried her.

"We weren't sure if she was the human in question or not." Krell followed closely, seemed to be moving at their side. "Her body isn't human any longer. She's not a cyborg but she's close or an updated design. We worried that she is a spy sent from Earth to track us with that human's information to use to gain our trust. We didn't want to notify you until we were certain of who or what she is because of your emotional association with her."

"Why is she ill?"

"She has implants inside her head and she stated she's been conditioned to hide her real identity. Hearing or saying that name causes pain and obvious violent physical symptoms." Krell spoke quickly. "Give her to me now."

"Go to hell," Mavo hissed. "Someone should have told me. It's her. I know it. Do you know who her father was? He—"

"Don't say it," Krell demanded. "You could set her off again. We're aware of who she stated her father was. Our creator."

"He could do this. It's her. It's my E—" He stopped. "It's her. What is she called now?"

"Cyan Eous."

Mavo halted and chuckled. "Of course. It's her favorite shade of blue."

"What?"

"She wanted her office painted," Mavo said as he continued to walk. "We debated over colors forever and that's the one she chose. It was a running joke between us. It's her, Krell. She's alive!"

"Stop," Krell demanded. "You're not taking her aboard the *Vontage*."

"I'm not letting her go."

Something rough happened, jerking Mavo hard to a stop, and hands gripped Cyan. "She's mine, Mavo. You can't have her. You have a female."

"She's a daughter to me. I'm not carrying her off to engage in sex," Mavo gasped.

"She's my female," Krell snarled. "I'm her primary male and the only one in her family unit. Release her to me this instant or we will fight to the death."

The arms holding her seemed to sag and her body was ripped away from Mavo. The hard body that gripped her in the cradle of firm arms was familiar as Krell snatched her away and violently turned, stomping as he moved.

"Bring her back!" Mavo came after them.

"Back off," Krell rasped. "She's mine and I'm not giving her up, even for you. Take it up with the council if you have a grievance but until that point, stay away from her! She's my female."

"Krell!"

He moved faster, nearly running with her, jostling her body in his arms, and Cyan fought to regain control of any part of her body. Her eyes wouldn't open, her limbs were flaccid, and while she was aware of everything, she couldn't do anything about it.

Mavo was alive, she'd held him, and she'd just learned that Krell and she were joined in a family unit, according to him. She was his female, he was her primary male—that obviously meant husband—and the shock of that information nearly made her pass out. *When was he going to tell me? That son of a bitch!*

Chapter Eleven

"Drink this," Krell ordered, pushing the warm cup closer to her lips.

Cyan glared at him. He'd taken her to Dell's old quarters, she assumed, since she'd never ventured there on her visits to the shuttle when the mercenary had owned it. It was a nice stateroom aboard the *Bridden*, probably the only private sleeping quarters on the small shuttle, and while it was compact, the bed was a double size.

"Please drink?" He sat on the edge of the soft mattress, grimly looking at her.

"When were you going to tell me we were married?"

He flinched. "You were conscious after your episode? You heard what was said between Mavo and me?"

"No. I'm a mind reader and guessed." She drew in a breath. "That's sarcasm. How could you not tell me? How? And why did you threaten to kill Mavo? He wasn't going to carry me off and have his way with me while I was down."

Anger tensed his mouth. "He was going to take you aboard the *Vontage* and planned to keep you away from me."

"That doesn't sound like a bad plan at this moment, you lying jerk! You accused me of being dishonest but you take the cake."

"Cake?" He set the cup on the small table next to the bed. "Could you please speak English?"

"Fine. You're a dick, Krell. You allowed the council to marry us, didn't even tell me, and have treated me as though I'm some devious spy bent on destroying cyborgs. That's a shitty way to treat your own wife." She took a deep breath. "How do we get a divorce? You better hide anything sharp if you say there isn't such a thing. I'm all for becoming a widow if that's what it takes."

"Calm down."

"Go to hell."

He watched her, frowning. "Cyan, it wasn't my idea. I wasn't the one who initiated sex between us."

"You said we could have it and not be married. You lied!"

"We were already joined into a family unit. You were assigned to me by the council when you were released from Medical." He paused. "Blame Councilman Zorus. He feared they would assign you to other males who would force the issue. I never would. We're both friends with Mavo and we wanted to protect you in case you really were that human he cared so deeply for from Earth." He paused again. "You're safe in my care. Have I ever forced you to suffer my unwanted touch? Have I allowed other males into a family unit with us? No."

She stared down at her hands, clutched together on her lap where she leaned against the padded headboard. She didn't even know what to say. She felt betrayed and angry. She'd been the one to go after Krell, couldn't deny that, but he should have told her they were married. It was just rude not to mention that detail. She inwardly snorted. *Understatement!* Pain came next. It hurt that he'd lied, had kept something so significant from

201

her, and he obviously wasn't thrilled either since he'd tried to resist her advances.

"Cyan?" His raspy voice lowered to a whisper. "Look at me."

She lifted her gaze. "What?"

"I'm worried about you. Are you well? How do you feel? May a medic examine you?"

"I'm fine."

"You were convulsing and lost consciousness."

"I wasn't totally passed out but my body shut down. I think being directly confronted and hearing those names from someone from my past caused that reaction. Names cause severe reactions. I heal fast and I'm sure no permanent damage was done. I don't even have a headache."

"May a medic examine you?"

"No."

Frustration flashed across his features. "I'm still worried. You frightened me."

"I'd probably care if you weren't such a dick." His concern did matter but she wasn't going to admit that to him. "I'm really fine. May I see Mavo now?"

"No." His fingers curled into fists. "You don't belong to him. He has a female in his family unit."

"He's my friend. I want to talk to him, not ball him."

"What?"

"Never mind. It's a graphic sex term. I just want to talk to my friend."

"No. We're almost done with the repairs and we're going to leave the planet's surface. You may see him once we reach Garden. I'll allow him to visit you in our home."

Her anger spiked. "You'll allow him? Really? Is that how you think it's going to work? That you have a say in who I see and who my friends are? You never answered me about a divorce. How do I obtain one?"

"I didn't mean it that way. You're seeking to start an argument."

"You're right. I'm mad!"

"I understand." His hands unclenched and he reached for her, paused, but dropped them to the bed inches from her leg. His gaze held hers. "You don't want to be separated from me, Cyan. They will assign you to another male if you protest our joining. The council isn't going to allow you to live without someone to protect you and to be your primary male. I won't harm you and I'd never force you to do anything you don't wish. I'm sorry I didn't tell you what had been done but I was hopeful that the situation would be resolved before you had to be informed. I wished to avoid upsetting you this way."

"What does that mean?"

"It is possible that you could be deemed human if you truly are who you claim to be before you were given that body. That means you'd be the female who helped cyborgs escape from Earth and you would be given special concessions."

"Now it's your turn to speak English."

"You'd be considered human regardless of your body's origins if I could prove you were the daughter of our creator. Cyborg law wouldn't apply to you and you wouldn't be required to take more than one male into a family unit. Humans are exempt from that law as long as they provide a child for the male of their choosing. In my case, I'm undesirable and no child is required by me. I'm not part of a breeding pact and my obligation has already been met by Mavo. He had a son and he's registered as my contribution to our future."

She took that information in. "He had a son for you, to cover your obligation?"

"Yes."

"You just threatened to kill him. Nice."

He flinched. "I was agitated. He was taking you away from me. I'll apologize later."

A nagging thought popped into her head. "Why did you care so much? You should have been happy to have someone want to take me off your hands."

He looked away to study the wall.

"Krell?"

"I need to see how things are progressing. Rest, Cyan. Lie down and please drink the healing tea. You've had a trauma. Stay put." He stood quickly, turned and strode to the door. "I'll return soon."

He fled and she sat there in stunned silence for a few minutes. He'd refused to answer her and that made her wonder why. Was he getting attached to her? Maybe he'd experienced jealousy when Mavo tried to carry her off? Was he feeling possessive? It opened all kinds of possibilities, most of which meant he cared more than his gruff exterior showed.

She carefully rose to her feet, tested her legs to make sure they worked and took a few deep breaths. She rolled her shoulders, shoved her braid out of the way and found her boots on the floor where Krell had placed them when he'd put her on the bed. She sat down, put them on and stood again. He was in for a rude awakening if he believed she'd meekly follow his orders just because they were married.

Her eyes closed as that information still stunned her. *I'm married to the grim cyborg*. She checked her clothes, made sure they were neat and approached the door. It opened and she was glad he hadn't tried to lock her inside. She was on the lower deck of the shuttle, near the cargo doors that led outside, and she turned in that direction. Something caught her attention as she stepped inside. Across the room near the open door her weapons had been neatly stored on the wall. She grinned.

Krell had distracted her the first time she'd left the shuttle with him and she'd missed seeing them. She quickly put on her belt and checked her weapons before returning them to the holsters down the front of her thighs. It made her feel more like her old self with them in place. It might get her shot when the cyborgs got a look at them but she didn't care. The planet had warlike inhabitants and from the amount of men sporting heavy-duty weapons, the threat wasn't just bullshit Krell had made up to keep her close.

The guard at the end of the ramp turned his head and his grip on his rifle blaster tightened as he faced her.

"Stand down," she ordered him with a smile. "I'm Krell's wife. He'd get pissed if you shoot me. You've met my husband and know he's not someone you want to mess with."

The cyborg frowned in response but he didn't point the weapon at her. That was good enough. She figured she might as well use her status to do what she wanted. Krell obviously didn't have a problem using his status as her primary male to issue orders since he'd taken her away from Mavo.

"Where did he go?"

Indecision made the guy hesitate. "To the *Vontage* to check on their repair status."

"That's where I'll be too." She walked down the ramp past him and rounded the shuttle. The sight of that big hotel on thrusters on the ground still wasn't something she'd adjusted to. It looked too weird. The feel of the baked ground under her boots made her step carefully, not wanting to slip and fall on her ass.

The *Vontage*'s underside was a hive of activity with repair teams working and men watching the surrounding thick vegetation. She glanced along the outline of ugly trees, wondering what could be so badass to make all those cyborgs look that nervous.

She'd been to alien planets a few times and hadn't seen anything too scary. Of course, by the time they visited a planet, settlers were already there and the military had been sent out to resolve some unrest between them. This planet hadn't been colonized. Her gaze drifted back to the men under the shade of the big ship. Krell wasn't too hard to spot with his tall frame and jet-black hair.

She nearly made it to him when a loud roar fractured the sounds of male voices as they worked. She halted, turned her head in the direction of the noise, and didn't see anything at first but trees. Another loud roar sounded, something ominous and deep, near thunderous, and the ground under her feet thumped.

What the hell? Her hands automatically grabbed the handles of her weapons.

"Incoming," a cyborg yelled. "Northeast section. Four annihilators are spotted."

Four what? The ground shook again, trembled as if something big had slammed against it, and the volume of the next roar nearly hurt her ears. She turned toward the teams of heavily armed cyborgs as all of them dropped to their bellies and aimed the biggest weapons they carried toward the trees. Backup cyborgs rushed forward with more crates, tore the lids open, yanked out weapons and rushed to lie down next to their fellow crew members.

Her heart raced and no one seemed to notice her in the chaos that followed. More cyborgs rushed toward the first wave of armed cyborgs, dropping down beside their crew until they formed a long line of men aiming weapons in the same direction.

The ground shook worse, huge thumps that made her brace her legs, and suddenly two of the trees were ripped apart. Something big just seemed to grab hold of the trunks, uproot them, and they sailed into the air to disappear into the thickly wooded area. The thing that stepped out made her back up.

"Holy fuck," she hissed, taking another step back.

The thing that came into view resembled something between a dinosaur with its massive body, stood two or three stories high, but had a humanoid-shaped torso with large, clawed limbs. The head of the thing was huge, had big black-looking round eyes in a furry face, and as its mouth opened, another roar tore from its vast, gaping jaws. Cyan could have sworn she felt the wind hit her face from that thing's anger as if it had expelled its breath that far.

The cyborgs opened fire to hit the ground in front of it. Explosions flashed, the noise earsplitting, and flames shot upward from the ground to form a wall between the creature and them. They missed the thing by a good forty feet.

Aim higher, she urged them silently. The creature turned and dived out of the way, disappearing into the line of thick trees, and the smoke from the bomb grenades they'd sent at it rose at that point to hide it.

"Cyan!" Krell grabbed her arm, drawing her attention. "Get inside the *Bridden*."

She gaped up at him. "What was that?"

"We call them annihilators. Return to the shuttle. The repairs aren't completed. We need another ten minutes." He gave her a gentle shove. "Run. I'm ordering it to lift off. It's too dangerous for you to remain here."

"They need to aim higher. They missed it."

"We don't wish to kill them unless we have to."

"Are you serious? Did you see that thing? It's huge and pissed!"

208

"They are just attempting to defend their planet."

Half of her admired the cyborgs for their compassion but the other half, the military soldier inside her, protested. "Will they stay back?"

"Doubtful. They'll come at us from different angles." He moved his big body enough for her to witness more cyborgs rushing from the *Vontage*, all carrying heavy-duty weapons, and they lay down to surround the ship and take positions to cover all directions. "Return to the *Bridden*." He glanced down at her body and his jaw clenched. "Now."

She released her weapons. "We're not going to blast off and abandon the other ship. Hand me one of those grenade launchers. I can handle them."

"It's not your fight."

"Bullshit!" Anger burned. "You've got hundreds of cyborgs on that ship, right? It's crippled and you need to buy it more time for the repairs to be finished. We're not abandoning them."

"I'm not. You're going on the *Bridden* and it will lift off to take you to safety." His hold on her arm tightened. "Move."

She twisted hard, grabbed his arm and ended up behind him. Her hand gripped his braid. "Don't fight with me, Krell. Don't make me kick your ass in front of your buddies."

She quickly released him, her point made, and jumped back. The ground under her shook and a roar came from the woods. She forgot their argument to turn her head in the direction of the sound. Trees split apart and another big beast rushed out. The ground shook noticeably as it ran at them, bigger than the *Bridden* they'd flown in on once she got a look at the long back of it. It had six legs, a huge torso, and those huge arms attached to a very wide chest. It also looked really angry.

The cyborgs fired, targeted the ground in front of it, and the ground blew apart in a fiery haze of hell. The thing roared again, more wind hitting her, and now she was certain those things were doing it. It retreated a little but didn't flee into the trees this time. It held its ground while glaring through the smoke and flames at them.

"Oh man," she whispered. "Ballsy or stupid."

"They are determined and fearless." Krell gripped her arm again. "I'm ordering you to return to the *Bridden* and the pilot is going to lift off the surface. I'll join you once we're back in orbit. I need to help but I want you safe, Cyan."

"Then stop wasting your time arguing with me." She jerked out of his hold and ran for the underbelly of the *Vontage*. A crate of launchers had been opened and she headed for them.

She peered inside at the weapons, spotted some other toys, and grinned when she grabbed the miclo twelve. She hadn't seen one in years but it had once been her favorite weapon of choice for creating mass havoc. The shell box for it sat at the bottom of the crate under it and she hoisted them up. She nearly turned into Krell's big body.

"Cyan," he snarled.

"Do you know what this is?"

He glanced at it. "No. We acquired some weapons recently from pirates who chose to attack the *Vontage*. They stole them from humans and we haven't tested that particular weapon yet, to my knowledge."

210

"Meet my old best friend. It's not my first choice but it will do. Move."

"We don't want to kill them."

"I heard you. Why aren't you using these? Do you have more? Find them and do something useful besides annoying me." She darted around him and ran for the line of cyborgs on the ground nearest her. She ignored Krell yelling her name.

She found a hole and dived between the cyborgs. The unforgiving ground made her wince when she landed on her belly. It was rough, hard and uncomfortable. She ignored the shocked cyborgs next to her as she set up the miclo's legs to make it a ground weapon and opened up the shell box, loading it quickly.

"What are you doing?"

She didn't glance at the cyborg to her right. "The enemy makes noise. This makes a louder one. Pass the word to cover your ears and do it fast."

The creature waited for the smoke and fire to clear before it began advancing. Cyan's hands shook slightly as she adjusted the sights on the gun and targeted the thing center-mass in the chest. She ignored the trembling ground as the big thing advanced, picking up speed as it ran at them. It would hurt the thing like a son of a bitch but it wouldn't kill it. She fired, released the weapon once it launched the shell and grabbed her ears.

"Fire in the hole!" she yelled, hoping the cyborgs heard her.

She kept her attention on the shell, a white ball the size of a flattened baseball on the back side with a point on the front side to help it fly through the air with accuracy, and her keen eyes tracked it until it hit the beast. The thing staggered back, opened its jaws, and the shell ruptured from the

211

impact. It wasn't as pretty as a grenade, no smoke or flames, but the sound was earsplitting, resembling a crack of thunder going off really close. The beast fell back, lay there and didn't move.

"You killed it," someone gasped.

"No." She shook her head. "I stunned it. Look at the right claw. It's just going to have a bruise from hell from the impact and a lasting headache." She reloaded another shell and was careful not to touch the still-hot barrel. "Meet the miclo twelve. It stands for something longwinded but we just dubbed them microphone louds or crowd busters. You set one of these babies off and everyone runs once they can get up after the splitting headache and having your bell rung through your eardrums. Anything within two hundred yards of impact is hit with intense sonic waves."

The beast on the ground kicked its legs and slowly rolled over to crawl toward the trees. Another one tried to enter the clearing and Cyan targeted it. She took aim and fired, covered her ears, and this time watched the cyborgs around her.

"Fire in the hole!" she yelled in warning.

The men grabbed their ears. She smiled, not glancing at the beast, but instead at their reactions when the shell hit the thing. The loud noise made some of the men wince and she finally glanced at the beast she'd targeted. It was down and not moving. The cyborg next to her shoved up to his feet.

"Get more of those weapons if we have them!"

"You're welcome," Cyan muttered, releasing her ears and reloading another shell.

212

Someone grabbed her belt and rudely hoisted her to her feet. An arm wrapped around her belly and she grunted when she hung in the air. Krell adjusted his hold on her, turning her to face him. He appeared furious when their gazes met.

"They have it. Let's go."

"Put me down!"

"No." He got in her face. He kept her off the ground, in his arms, locked tightly in his embrace. "Enough. You've made your point and put yourself in danger."

She gripped his shoulders and her nose nearly brushed his. "I can help."

"I don't want you to."

It hurt her feelings. "You have weapons you didn't even know what to do with. You might not want my help but you need it. If you own Earth weapons, you should know what the hell they are and learn how they work."

He growled at her.

She itched to slap him just for manhandling her. She could force him to put her down but she'd have to inflict serious damage. She didn't want to do that, not to him. Instead her fingers tightened on the curve of his shoulders.

"You could have been killed if that stunt hadn't worked. It was running at you." He breathed heavily and his blue eyes appeared black from anger. "I would have watched you be trampled. That's what they do. They smash anything in their path, throw it or batter it to death."

213

His words made some of her anger recede. He was genuinely scared for her safety. He showed it by appearing extremely livid but she'd seen men worry about her before and he had it bad. Some guys channeled their fear into raw rage and Krell obviously happened to be one of them.

"I'm fine." She eased her grip on him and rubbed his tense muscles instead.

"Fire in the hole," a male yelled as a miclo fired.

Cyan grabbed Krell's ears to cover them instead of her own since both of his arms were around her waist holding her body against him and buried her face in the crook of his neck. One of her ears pressed against his throat and the other tight to her inner arm. The loud noise was muted enough not to hurt when it came.

His body tensed and he turned quickly and headed toward the *Bridden*. She released his ears and lifted her head. He didn't look at her, instead watched where they were going, and she didn't fight to be put down. The cyborgs had the weapons to use against the oncoming beast things. She'd helped and that was all that really mattered.

"I'm a soldier, Krell."

He glanced at her, his mouth set in a grim line, and he swallowed hard enough that the scars on his throat flexed from his bobbing Adam's apple. "Not anymore. You're mine to protect and I will even if that means I have to restrain you to a bed to keep you safe."

She licked her lips. "It sounds kinky."

He glanced at her again, growled deep in his throat, and kept advancing toward the shuttle at a quick pace. Cyan lifted her legs and

214

wrapped them around his waist since he seemed hell bent on carrying her. It made it easier for him to do and her legs weren't bumping against his. She felt his hard-on instantly and grinned. Either danger gave him wood or his thoughts were going where hers had at his threat of how to keep her out of trouble.

Every step he took ground his cock against her pussy and by the time he reached the cargo area of the *Bridden* she was turned-on too. Danger always made her heart race, firing guns was exciting and the high of adrenaline was a pure rush. The fact that the sexy cyborg was being so forceful also pushed her arousal buttons. So few men ever attempted it with her and he did it so well.

He stomped through the cargo room into the corridor and his arm left her waist to open the stateroom door. It closed behind him and she gasped when Krell spun to press her back against the bulkhead, pinning her between the solid wall and his firm body. Their gazes met.

"I am furious."

Cyan lunged for his mouth, surprising him enough that his lips parted as he gasped and she had her in. Her tongue delved inside, her hands slid into his constrained hair and she wished it were free. She'd love to fist handfuls of the silky strands. She kissed him for all she was worth and was overjoyed when he responded with equal passion.

She burned with desire, wished they were naked and that he was already inside her as his hips ground against her pelvis. His cock was trapped inside his pants but he still rubbed against the inner seam of her pants to tease her clit. Krell took control of the kiss, not something that surprised her since he liked to be in charge in the bedroom.

He turned, pulled her away from the wall, and walked a few steps until he bumped into something. They fell, his arms left her and he braced his weight to avoid crushing her when they hit the bed with her under him. The soft mattress cushioned her fall.

Cyan tore her mouth from his. "Get naked."

The blue of his eyes seemed to show that his anger faded while he stared at her. He licked his lips. She followed the movement of his tongue and regretted they weren't still kissing. The guy knew how to curl her toes.

"Don't make me beg. I've mentioned it's not pretty."

"I would wager it's extremely sexy."

His words made her smile. "Lift off me."

He hesitated but did it, pushed away from her, and she released him to allow their bodies to separate. He backed up and stood at the end of the bed. Cyan grabbed her shirt, tugging at it, and sat up. She tore her shirt over her head, removed her sports bra next and nudged him with her boot.

"Back up a little more."

He breathed heavily, was turned-on, and his pants revealed his cock stretching out the front of them. He took a few steps away and she bent, tore at her boots and just dropped them on the floor. She stood, removed her belt with her weapons still inside their holsters, and unfastened her pants, shoving them down quickly. Her gaze lifted as she stepped close to him, completely naked, her hands going for his tank top.

"Raise your arms."

He growled at her. "I don't take orders well."

"Please?" She fluttered her eyelashes at him playfully and grinned. "Raise your arms."

He lifted them and she tore his shirt up to reveal his sexy torso, the scars on his chest, and her mouth latched onto a nipple. His body tensed, swayed in response, and he helped her shove his shirt off when her arms couldn't take it any higher up his tall frame. It fell to the floor somewhere. Her hands dropped to the front of his pants, frantically tearing them open.

"Slow down," Krell rasped.

She sucked hard on him, her teeth lightly nipped at the taut peak, and his hands gripped her hips in response. She pulled her mouth off and took a step back to lower his pants. She wasn't going to mess with his boots or even remove the damn things. She wanted him now.

She freed his cock, a beautiful, impressive sight of firm flesh that she wanted buried deep inside her body as fast as possible, but Krell had thought seeing her beg would be sexy. She didn't want to disappoint. She wasn't one to beg but she could compromise as she gripped his bare hips, slid her hands to push the pants down his thighs and dropped to her knees before him. Her fingernails lightly scored his skin as she slid them toward the front of his hips, wrapped one hand around the thick base of his shaft and lifted her chin to peer up at him.

Krell had dropped his chin, his eyes narrowed as he watched her intensely and he appeared a little flushed from excitement, making his features a dusky hue. His chest rose and fell rapidly, his breathing increased and she didn't look away as she opened her mouth to run her tongue over her lips.

"What are you doing?" His husky confusion was sexy.

"What does it look like?"

He frowned. "Examining me? I'm healthy."

Her mind reeled and shock hit her hard. "Krell, honey, has anyone ever gone down on you before?" *It can't be. No way!*

He said nothing but his features closed down. All expression faded and she was pretty sure she had her answer. "Damn cyborg women. I need to have a talk with them. I guess when you have your pick of men clamoring for your attention you get to be pretty selfish in the sack. They are missing out."

She licked her lips again, opened her jaw wider and glanced at his cock. She inched closer. He was big, thick, but she was willing to try to fit him inside her mouth. She licked the crown, running her tongue around the rim, and heard him hiss. She resisted the grin that threatened to surface and wrapped her lips around him. Her mouth tightened, careful of her teeth, and she began to slowly move on him, taking a few inches inside.

"Cyan," he groaned.

She was guessing that was a good way to say her name. He wasn't pulling away or trying to stop her. One of his hands brushed her shoulder gently, a caress, almost as if he were afraid to touch her. She made a mental note to seriously have a talk with cyborg women if they didn't do this for guys. *It should be a two-way street. To get, you should also give oral sex. Sex 101 and they need to learn it.* She pushed those thoughts back as the

218

taste of him penetrated her senses and she moaned around him. The sweetness of his pre-cum was surprising and pleasant.

She heard his breathing change to a harsh pant while she worked him inside her mouth, sucking and teasing his seriously rigid cock. She took more until it threatened to choke her when the crown of his sex reached the back of her throat. She turned her head, taking him at different angles, and his hand actually gripped her shoulder, a warning that he was close to coming.

At first she thought she'd just do it long enough to get him really turned-on but that was before she realized he'd never had someone give him head. Now she wanted to finish what she started. She moved faster, her free hand grabbed his muscular ass to keep him still in case he tried to pull away at the last second, and she grew a little rougher with her mouth.

"Cyan," he snarled, trying to gently step back.

Her hand on his ass tightened, her fingernails dug in just enough to be a warning and then he was coming. His body shook as the sweet taste of his cum filled her mouth. She swallowed each burst, keeping him tightly in her hold with her lips and tongue and slowed the pace just enough to milk him until his climax ended. She pulled off him carefully, licked her lips and released his cock to grab his hip instead. She used his body to pull herself to a standing position.

Krell's head hung forward until his chin rested against his chest, his eyes closed, and he panted. A sheen of sweat slickened his body as if he'd been running.

She smiled, watched him recover, until his eyelashes parted. "That wasn't exactly begging but it's as close as I get. I was on my knees."

Chapter Twelve

Cyan gasped when Krell suddenly gripped her arms and knocked her on her ass to land on the bed. She hadn't seen that coming and as her body bounced on the mattress, she was even more stunned when he dropped to his knees, grabbed her under her calves and lifted her legs, putting her flat on her back with them in the air. He hoisted her ass to the edge of the mattress with his hold on her, jerked her thighs far apart and bent forward.

His mouth locked over her clit before she realized what he'd done, firm lips sealed around the bundle of nerves and his tongue pressed firmly against it. He growled, adding vibration to the wonderful sensation, and his tongue played hell as he rubbed it furiously against the spot that made her cry out.

She clawed at the bedding, just for something to hold on to, and pure pleasure tore through her. He had no mercy, using his mouth and tongue to make her pant. She tried to move her hips, needed to, but he pressed his forehead against her lower belly to hold her down. He growled again, sucked a little while he mastered her clit and Cyan realized she'd beg him to continue if he stopped. She was going to come fast and intensely if he kept it up and she really wanted to go over that edge.

Her body tensed, her back arched, pushing her pussy tighter against his wonderful mouth and strong tongue, and she forgot how to breathe, holding air inside her lungs. It only heightened the pleasure. Her nails dug into the bedding, clawed it, and air filled her lungs finally as she screamed out Krell's name when sheer ecstasy struck. The climax brutally tore through her body, shooting straight from his tongue to her brain.

He tore his mouth away and her back dropped to the mattress. Her vaginal walls twitched from the strength of her release, warmth spread through her belly and she gasped as his cock suddenly entered her in one strong, driving thrust. His thick, rigid shaft sank into her deeply and his weight came down, pinned her, and her eyes opened.

Krell stared at her, not moving, their bodies locked together, and he adjusted his hold on her. One hand gripped her ass to lift her hips a little tighter against his, urging her with a motion to wrap her legs around his waist, which she did. His other hand cupped her face before he lowered his until their mouths nearly brushed.

"You could have died out there."

"You're still on that?" Her legs tightened, urging him to move. "It's over."

"We are not."

She paused, letting his words sink in. "I meant the situation outside is over. At least I hope it is since one of those things isn't batting this shuttle around. I wasn't talking about you and me."

"Good." His fingertips slid into her hair. "I didn't welcome you into my life at first but you're an integral part of it now."

She wasn't sure how to take that. It made her heartbeat a little erratic though, an indication that it mattered way too much. She wanted to know what he meant though.

"Krell?"

His gaze dropped to her mouth before he looked up again. "Cyan?"

She grinned, enjoying his sense of humor, which he showed at odd moments. "What do you want from me besides this?"

"This?"

"Sex. Are we more? Where do you want this to go?"

Krell's mind stumbled a little at Cyan's question. He didn't have an immediate answer to give. At first he'd wanted to be rid of her as quickly as possible but that was before she'd taken him on in a physical challenge at his home. Finding his face planted in a mat with her pinning him down had woken something inside him that he'd never known existed. She surprised him, made him admire her courage and fearlessness, and it had been entirely too pleasant.

He'd been sure she'd planned to use her alluring body to bypass his suspicious nature but she hadn't acted the way he'd expected. He genuinely believed she wanted him, despite his flaws, and her responses to his touch were far too genuine to be an act. She was his female, his woman, and watching her hug Mavo had made him realize how easily he could lose her to another male.

Jealousy wasn't something he experienced but it was an emotion he'd learned well since Cyan had entered his life. As petty as he believed it would be, he knew he didn't want to share her, didn't want another male to touch her and only wanted her to look at him the way she did at that moment. Her passion-softened features were so beautiful to him.

He wanted to keep her. Period. No doubt about it. He'd fight and kill any male who attempted to lure her from him. He'd battle the council if they refused to give her special concessions. Mavo believed she truly was the daughter of their creator and that had a good chance of being enough proof to sway their confidence in the matter. He no longer cared if she was Emily Pleva or a spy pretending to be her. Cyan Eous was his female, he was her primary male, and her true identity was irrelevant. *She's mine.*

He studied her expressive eyes, the blue of them drawing him in as she waited for him to answer. The words were difficult to form. He didn't want her to grow smug about his deep-seated attachment, to take advantage of his weakness for her, and doubted she'd respect a male who wished to adore her.

He bit back a groan, his cock stiffening more inside her tight pussy that gripped his shaft in a heavenly embrace. His mouth had just worshiped her and he wanted to do it again. The memory of her responses, the sounds she made and her taste made the list of highlights of his lifetime.

Krell took a slow breath. He'd be firm in his resolve to keep her by making his stance known. He'd leave no doubt in her mind that he wouldn't allow her to walk away from him and that he planned to keep her. Some of the tension eased from his body. They were both strong individuals and he'd have to remember that. He just hoped most of their battles of wills ended up the way this one had. He fought a grin. He looked forward to baiting her if that was how Cyan settled arguments.

Cyan hated it when Krell didn't answer, dreading that he was about to shoot down any possibility that they might have something lasting and real. She'd always kept her heart safe but he had a way of getting to her as no other man ever had. He knew what and who she really was, even if he didn't fully believe it, but she figured since Mavo he might have changed his mind about being so distrustful of her.

"You wish to discuss this now?" His voice came out smooth and steady.

"I'm curious."

"I'm your primary male."

"My husband." The word was still surprising to work her mouth around. She'd gotten married and hadn't even known it.

"Yes." He adjusted his weight to ease some of it off her chest. "I am. You're my female."

"Where does that leave us?"

"Permanently together." He ran his tongue over his bottom lip and his teeth dented it.

She stared deeply into his eyes, trying to read him but couldn't guess his emotions. He was really good at hiding them when he wanted to. He stopped biting his mouth and took a deep breath, his chest pressing against hers as he inhaled.

"I won't release you. I'll protest if you request the council to dissolve our family unit." Anger flashed across his handsome, scarred face at that point. "You wanted me and you have me, Cyan. This isn't a game. State your intentions now."

My intentions? Did he really just say that?

"Are you planning to protest our family unit?"

"I–"

The door to the room suddenly slid open and an unknown cyborg entered. "We're under attack!"

Krell jerked his head around, his body shielding Cyan's from the view of the other male. "The inhabitants?"

"No. An enemy shuttle is hovering. It is the one that attacked us in space."

"Shit!" Cyan shoved at Krell's chest to allow her to get up. "The Markus Models found us."

"Affirmative," the cyborg verified, his gaze averted. "They are threatening to open fire on the *Vontage* if we don't surrender. They are stating they have backup on the way."

"I'll be right there."

The cyborg spun around, rushing out of the room. Krell abruptly shoved away, his body withdrew from hers, and he frantically dressed. Cyan lunged up, scooted for the end of the bed and leaned down to grab her own clothing.

"Stay put," Krell harshly ordered her. "We'll have to battle them from the ground." Fury gripped his features. "I should have been at my post, alert to the danger, but instead I was distracted by you. This is my fault."

"How could you have known they'd find us, Krell? I'm sure you evaluated the odds, it's what you do. Don't blame yourself. A ground fight

226

would be suicide. Hovering means they already have every weapon they possess trained on both ships and they'll be targeted with the planetary missiles those shuttles have to be equipped with. We're not in space. The shielding on our ships isn't designed to protect against them, Krell."

He turned at the door, tearing his shirt down over his chest. "We have no choice. We can't be taken alive to be tortured until some break. The Markus Models can't discover the location of Garden. We'll fight to the death and blow our own ships up before we allow them to be captured and used to figure out where we've been traveling."

"Stall them. We'll think up something, Krell."

He still hesitated. "I am deeply sorry, Cyan. I failed to keep you safe. This is entirely my fault."

The doors opened and he was gone. She cursed a blue streak as she yanked on her own clothing, fumbled for her weapons belt and shoved on her boots. A ground war with a military shuttle outfitted for battle the way the Genesis Fours were would be pure stupidity. The Markus Models would disable both ships easily, trap the cyborgs on the planet and just capture them off one by one if the big beast things didn't kill them first.

"Shit!" She left the room but instead of heading toward the cargo area, she rushed to the pilot station. A plan began to form as she hit the lift to take her to the higher level. "Damn cyborgs and metal heads. Both stubborn and mule headed."

She dropped into the pilot's seat and opened communications. Her heart pounded and fear gripped her. Krell would die if she couldn't pull off this insane stunt. Mavo too, along with hundreds of cyborgs. The Markus

Models would hand them over to Earth Government and they'd be slaughtered in testing labs, be taken apart and examined, if they weren't murdered outright on sight. Not that the cyborgs would allow themselves to be captured alive. She forced all emotion out of her voice.

"Brothers," she stated calmly. "You have come to rescue your sisters. Respond to us. We're unable to link to you. Barcarintellus has boxed most of our functions and we are unable to override."

She closed her eyes, prayed a little, but they flew open when the coms clicked open. "Who is speaking?"

The familiar Markus Model voice sent chills down her spine. They hadn't altered their original ones. She'd hated talking to them when she'd had to interview the ones inside the plant, the one on Belta Station really had pissed her off and now she had to pretend to be one. It rankled her in the worst way.

"Your sisters. We are the female production line of the Markus Model," she lied. "We escaped to seek you but were located by cyborgs first. You have come to rescue us, brothers."

The hesitation was long. "Prove the association."

Her mind worked quickly, drawing from a conversation she'd had with a Markus at the plant they'd escaped from, before she'd left on her mission. She repeated the exact words one of them had said to her, pretty sure it was their motto in life. "We are sentient, superior to the infestation called humanity, and survival is our prime objective."

"What are your numbers?"

"We are four," she lied. "What are your numbers?"

"We are eight."

Eight of those damn things. She clenched her teeth. *That's not so bad. At least it's not fifty.*

"Twenty-three more of us will be arriving soon. We've come to interrogate the cyborgs for their base location and box them. We have made a deal with Earth Government for the freedom of our production line. Do you know the base location?"

"Affirmative," she lied. "One of us will come to you to share the coordinates."

"Transmit it."

"Unable to do so," she kept her voice cool, robotic. "Unable to transmit. We are damaged. One will share the location by directly linking to you with physical contact." She hoped it would confuse the damn things enough to get them to land and give her the opportunity to get close to them. "We are sending one out to you to share the location." Her fingers touched her weapons. It would probably be suicide but if she could cause severe damage to the inside their shuttle before they killed her, it would buy the cyborgs time to escape. "We're sending one now." She stood and turned.

Krell had a weapon aimed straight at her chest with four other cyborgs behind him, also pointing weapons at her body. The pain in his eyes was easy to read. She held his gaze and reached back, ending the transmission.

"I knew it," he rasped.

"Trust me, Too Tall."

"I did." His silvery skin was unusually pale, almost a pasty gray at that moment. "You're one of them."

"No, I'm not. They will allow me to walk onto their shuttle. Think about it."

His jaw clenched. "I can't trust you."

It hurt. "Do you have any better ideas? They aren't going to just allow us to fly out of here. Think, Krell. I am. I can prove I'm not human to them. I told you I can confuse them. Best-case scenario, they will shut down to analyze me long enough to buy me time to kill them. Worst case, I'm inside their shuttle and can target the interior enough to cripple it while you fly out of here. I don't know how long you were standing there but twenty-three more of them are coming. You analyze plans. Do your job and you'd know I'm right. This is a good plan and we're in deep shit. It's the best chance we've got to get out of this mess."

Krell forced his mind to work. The shock of being told Cyan was in contact with the enemy shuttle had sent him rushing back inside the *Bridden*. He'd managed to catch the last part of her conversation and he'd been staggered by the concept that she was one of a female line of the androids. He never would have guessed. A hybrid cyborg, definitely, but completely artificial in intelligence? *Never!*

He backed away from all his emotions, closed them off completely and separated them from Cyan. He did his job and that meant analyzing data and her plan. It was a solid one with a higher chance of success than a ground attack. Her odds of dying were excessively high, the probability of

230

her winning a battle facing off against eight androids even with her enhanced body was slim. She did have a good likelihood of crippling the interior of the shuttle if they allowed her entrance.

She'd die if the Markus Models attacked her. Emotions rushed back through him, striking as if someone punched him in various parts of his body. He waged his own battle silently. Hundreds of cyborg lives were on the line, more of the androids were on their way to the planet and time wasn't something he had much of. He'd have to make a decision now. He'd either have to trust her and allow her to execute her plan, one he had to admire for sheer courage, or he'd have to believe she wasn't a sentient being.

Krell stared into her eyes, saw pain flash inside them and knew with every fiber of his soul that she experienced true emotions. She wasn't just a sex bot some computer technician had programmed to act human. She was Cyan, his female, and it came down to allowing her to risk her life to save the lives of hundreds of cyborgs. Emily Pleva's body had changed but she had not. She was willing to save them once again.

He wanted to refuse, to strip her of the weapons on her belt and toss her over his shoulder to carry her off and restrain her to a bed. It wouldn't keep her safe though. They were trapped on the planet's surface, all but captured, and a quick death would be preferable for her than the horrors that awaited them on Earth. He'd read Councilman Zorus' report of how humans were fascinated with cyborgs' lack of aging. They'd planned to cut him apart while he was still alive. Cyan didn't age either and she contained advanced technology they didn't possess. Earth would be just as cruel to her, if not more so. She'd lived amongst them for decades without their knowledge and humans would take that as a high insult to their intelligence over being fooled.

Regret and shame filled him. He'd brought her on this mission, put her in danger, and now she'd pay the price for his mistake. He'd never forgive himself if he survived and she didn't. He would never recover if he lost her. They stared at each other and his weapon lowered. He turned his head to glare at his men.

"Holster your weapons."

The cyborgs hesitated but followed his order. He turned back and stared at her, wanting to memorize everything about her. Cyan slowly stepped forward, staring up at him. She reached for his face but he jerked back to avoid the brush of her fingertips on his skin. He didn't deserve her touch. He'd failed her and all he could do was make sure she succeeded in her mission, even if that happened to be allowing her to die. It was an honorable and worthy way to do so for the beautiful soul she possessed.

"Get both ships ready to lift off." Pain rolled through Cyan at Krell's rejection as her hand dropped to her side. "Is the *Vontage* able to fly yet?"

"Yes. The repairs are finished." Krell's voice sounded harsh to her.

She nodded. "They didn't say when the other Markuses are arriving. The important part is they don't get your people. It's been nice knowing you if I manage to blow up their shuttle."

His mouth clenched. "Your plan might work. It is insane enough to be considered genius."

She dropped her gaze and inched past him. The burn of tears nearly blinded her. He didn't completely trust her but he was allowing her to leave the *Bridden* to meet with the Markus Models. That had to count for something. She passed more cyborgs who had probably overheard her transmission and rushed to stop her from giving away Garden's location. She hadn't ever checked the shuttle's logs to try to trace it and wouldn't be a security risk if the Markus Models attempted to torture the location of it from her if she were captured.

She paused at the cargo doors and checked her weapons before glancing around. She found an ugly black tarp that would work as she tied it around her waist to hide her thighs, making a horrible fashion statement with the skirt and leggings look that clashed with her boots. One more deep breath and she walked out of the hold of the *Bridden*, purposely moving her limbs stiffly to appear less human.

The sight of the scarred Genesis Four shuttle hovering between the *Vontage* and the shuttle she exited made her hold back a smile. She'd dented it a bit on the belly—deep blemishes ran the length of it after their tussle in space and scorch marks showed near one thruster. The shuttle lowered slightly, about eight feet closer to her but kept away from the ground and the lower docking door opened. She waited and realized they issued their first test. Ten feet separated the glassy ground from the bottom of the ramp.

She took a deep breath, walked closer until she was under the opening they'd created and she dropped into a one-kneed crouch. Her legs tensed, her fingers flexed, and she stared up, calculating. She pushed up hard and fast, every muscle strained and she leapt. Her hands caught the thick metal edge of the ramp, gripped hard, and she pulled her body higher. No human could do that.

She managed to get her upper body high enough to lift her leg, hooked her knee on the ramp and climbed onto it. She straightened to her feet, stiffened her spine, and lifted her chin. Two Markus Models stood in the shadows watching her with interest. She noticed they stayed out of fire range of anyone on the ground as she purposely cocked her head at an odd angle, slowly advancing on them.

"Brothers."

The ramp under her started to lift to close and she kept advancing. Her gaze swept the cargo area, verifying they were alone. Six of them weren't present. The two Markuses approached as soon as the ramp sealed closed. They marched in unison to stop a few feet in front of her. Both of them watched her with dead eyes. It scared her but she hoped she hid her fear.

"Sister?" They didn't sound certain as they spoke at the same time, identically.

They sound as creepy as hell. "Should we give you proof?" She remembered to talk in the plural, not to give herself away.

"Yes," they both stated.

She smiled, wondering how they'd react at her next words. "I brought you a puppy to play with." The second the words were out, she launched a physical attack. One hand shot out to hit the one to her right in the face, aiming for his eyes with her clawed hand since they were made out of organic material and would blind him, while she targeted the other with her leg to knock him back to give her precious seconds. Her hand tore at the skirt, ripped it away and jerked her gun free from the holster.

Cyan fired, shooting the one she had clawed, and dived to the left, her other hand going for her second gun as her back slammed onto the cargo deck when she flipped in the air as she fell. It seemed to stun them that she could move that fast since she was able to sink bullets in both of them before they recovered. She opened fire with the energy gun, nailing one of them before the twin model grabbed her. She pressed the muzzle of the weapon against its body as it landed over hers and pulled the trigger. She shoved it away when it convulsed.

She climbed to her feet, shot both of the downed, still twitching units and the smell of burning wires filled her nostrils. She figured the other six Markuses were more than aware she'd just taken out two of their brothers and she wasn't what she had claimed to be. Her gaze frantically searched for something to damage that would cripple the shuttle. No targets were visible.

The cargo doors to the interior of the shuttle didn't slide open and they didn't attack. That worried her but she didn't have time to ponder it. They could target the *Vontage* and *Bridden* with the shuttle's weapons. She rushed toward the doors to seek them out first.

She encountered the first set of Markuses a few feet from the door. They stood immobile, staring into space, and she fired a bullet into each of their faces. Glee hit her. The damn things were motionless because they were analyzing her as she'd hoped would happen—they had frozen in the process. *I just might make it out of this mess alive after all*. She nailed them with two energy shots that left both crumpled in a smoking heap of tangled limbs. She had four more to find and had to work fast, before their analysis completed and they regained function.

The third set stood motionless in an open lift, probably on their way down to greet her, and she took them out easily. She checked her bullets, wishing she had more as she searched the lower deck. She dragged out the destroyed Markuses and prepared for battle as the lift took her to the upper deck of the shuttle.

The last two Markuses were seated in the pilot seats. They didn't move at her approach and she didn't give them time to recover. She fired two shots to the back of each head, exposing the metal. She was happy to introduce the energy shots in rapid succession. The things smoked bad, making her wave her hand in front of her face and choke a little on the smell of burning, artificial hair. It stank nearly as bad as the real thing.

She grabbed each body and dragged them away from the seats. They were fried, their eyes turning white, and she dropped into the pilot seat. She hurried to set the shuttle on the ground, cut the engines, and took the shuttle's weapons offline. The urge to get off their ship fast gripped her strongly. She'd leave the bodies for the cyborgs to deal with. They could cut the Markus Models up into tiny pieces for all she cared or abandon them with the shuttle on the surface when they fled.

She moved quickly to rush to the lift, the fear finally hitting her hard at what she'd done, and all she could think about was Krell. She wanted to hug him, show him that he could trust her, and now he'd have to know once and for all that she wasn't the enemy. She'd just saved a lot of cyborgs from the Markus Models.

It seemed to take forever as she tapped her thigh, waiting for the cargo door to open at ground level, her eyes on the two downed Markuses, and they freaked her out. They were fried but she hoped to never see the things again. She rushed down the ramp as soon as the door hit the hard ground and came to a shocked halt.

"No!" Her legs collapsed under her and her knees painfully slammed into the glassy ground.

She couldn't believe what she saw but the view didn't change. The area around her was empty to the tree line surrounding the large, open space. The *Vontage* and *Bridden* were gone. They'd lifted off the surface and had left her behind. Krell had abandoned her.

Chapter Thirteen

"Cyan!"

The deep rumble of Krell's raspy voice jerked her head up and she gaped at him in astonishment. He moved fast, rushed at her from the side of the shuttle and she took in his appearance.

He had various weapons strapped to his body, including a miclo twelve slung by the strap over one broad shoulder and a grappling-hook gun gripped firmly in his fist. Surprise at the sight of him immobilized her until he crouched before her, his free hand cupped her face and his dark-blue eyes searched her wide gaze.

"Where are they? Are you well?"

"I thought you left me." Her voice broke and she had to clear her throat.

He frowned in response. "I ordered both ships to lift off the planet while you distracted the Markus Models but once the *Bridden* is certain the *Vontage* gets away without hindrance, it will return for us." He dropped the grappling gun. "I no longer need that. I planned to use it to attempt to gain access to the shuttle to help you."

Tears filled her eyes. He had stayed behind to try to rescue her. She reacted by lunging at him, throwing her arms around his neck, and nearly knocked him over in the process. He managed to catch her weight and keep his balance. His strong arm hugged her around her waist.

"Are you injured? Where are the Markus Models, Cyan?"

She sniffed against his throat, her nose pressed there. The grim cyborg had ordered his men to leave him behind on a hostile planet for the slim chance he might be able to break into a shuttle and fight at her side. It was suicidal and irrational, the worst plan ever for an analyst to make, yet he'd done it for her.

"They are all dead aboard the shuttle," she informed him, attempting to pull her frayed emotions together. "Fried and smoking, just the way they should be."

"You're certain?"

"Yeah." She nodded against him, hugging him tighter. "You didn't abandon me."

His arm tightened. "I wouldn't do that. You're my female, Cyan."

She hoped he hadn't hatched his crazy scheme out of some sense of responsibility as her assigned male but she was more than willing to take a leap of faith that she meant more to him than that. His plan had been flat-out irrational, the odds of it working were downright silly, but he'd stayed behind anyway.

A distant roar interrupted their reunion and Cyan released him. "Sounds as though the natives are recovering and possibly thinking of coming at us again."

Krell eased his hold on her while they separated. "Yes. We should lift off if the shuttle is operational and wait in orbit for the *Bridden* to return. They can dock with this to pick us up."

"Forget that. We don't need to be picked up." She glanced at his handsome face, feeling pure happiness that he was there with her. "We're now the proud owners of a Genesis Four shuttle. Do you know how bad I wanted to get my hands on the controls of one of these babies? Let's dump out the trash and lift off before those creatures decide to rush us."

Krell slowly released her and stood, pulling her to her feet in the process. He gripped the miclo and held it out to her. "You keep watch and I'll deal with the remains of the Markus Models. I don't wish to take them with us."

"That's the trash I was referring to. They give me the creeps. Two are in the cargo area, you'll find four more on your way to the lift, and the final two I dragged out of the piloting seats."

He hesitated, stared into her eyes and nodded. "I'll hurry." His gaze left hers to search the surrounding area. "You'll be fine and I'll work with speed. I'd prefer to leave their remains on the surface as well."

"Please hurry."

He ran up the ramp and Cyan kept her gaze roaming the tree lines, her feet sensitive to any ground movement since those things were heavy enough to cause it to quake when they moved. Another roar came from a new direction and she wished Krell would work faster. The idea of taking on more of those beast creatures wasn't something she wanted to do twice in a day, especially since she didn't have extra shells to fire at them.

A dragging sound drew her attention and she turned her head just in time to watch Krell shove two bodies off the side of the ramp at the top where the cargo bay opened. The limp Markus Models thudded on the ground. Krell disappeared from sight and she glanced at one of the bodies to see a hole in the back of its head. He'd gone after the ones in the piloting area first.

Krell was strong, dragging the androids two at a time, until all eight Models had been dumped on the barren surface of the planet. Cyan rushed into the shuttle, eager to lift off, and Krell closed the ramp to seal it. They moved together, side by side, with her nearly running to keep pace with his longer legs.

"I totally get to pilot, right?" She stared up at him when the doors of the lift that would carry them to the upper level closed. "Come on, Krell. Say yes."

He smiled. "You may pilot, Cyan."

She grinned. "I would have wrestled you for it."

His smile faded and his eyes narrowed. "You deserve to do whatever you wish. Your plan was effective and you saved my people."

She'd take gratitude at that moment if it meant getting her way. The second the lift doors opened, she rushed forward to drop into the pilot's seat. Krell took the one next to her and she studied the console.

"Oh man, this is so awesome. Top of the line."

"Cyan?" Krell motioned to one of the monitors. "Please lift off."

She followed his finger and grabbed for the controls. One of the creatures had started tossing trees their way. They landed far from the shuttle but the fact that it was trying to hit them wasn't lost on her. The inhabitants were leery to enter the barren area after losing their initial battle but they hadn't called it quits. She turned on the engines, powered up and engaged the thrusters.

"This may be a little rough."

Krell reached for his belts. "Why?"

"It's one thing to fly these in space but another to break through an atmosphere." She grinned. "I'm kidding. I've got this." *I hope.* She kept that part to herself. After walking into a shuttle manned by eight Markus Models, adjusting the speed and trajectory not to avoid shaking apart or burning up when leaving a planet should be a breeze.

She punched the thrusters and the shuttle shot upward at an accelerated speed. Krell softly muttered something.

"Sorry. The controls are pretty touchy. I'll get the hang of it."

"It would be awkward to die breaking atmosphere after what we've just survived."

She laughed and shot him a glance as she steered the shuttle higher, learning how to handle it as they rose through the green clouds. "Yeah. It would be."

He smiled as their gazes met. "I trust you."

She had to look away to watch the monitors, hated that the shuttle only had exterior cameras, and held back tears. It really touched her that he'd said those three words. *Now if I could only get him to say three more wonderful words.*

That thought sobered her. She was in love with him. No doubt about it. Krell had gotten under her skin, through her defenses, and it wasn't a great mystery how he'd done it. He knew what she was and he still wanted her. For once in her life she belonged to someone. When they touched it was more than sex, and while they had a lot of issues, she wanted to work them out.

The shuttle vibrated as she steered them into space. She breathed out a sigh of relief when they safely made the transition. Her gaze instantly sought out the monitor to make sure they were alone and cringed when it registered two dots.

"We're not alone. The question is, are they heading toward us or away from us?"

Krell leaned over, studying the same monitor. "Approaching."

"Shit! They are too far out to identify but I'm guessing it's not the *Vontage* and the *Bridden*."

"No." Krell sounded grim. "The *Vontage* is making a run for Garden and the *Bridden* was going to escort it a safe distance to make sure it wasn't being pursued before they return."

"I'm not good at remote hacking. Can you handle the shuttle's onboard computer in case they try to gain control of it?" Cyan pulled up the space charts to discover their location, found it, and studied where they were. "I think I can lose them in that moon cluster if we can reach it. Send out a warning signal to the *Bridden* if you're able to tell them not to return for us. I don't want them flying into a trap. They are out of range of our radar but their coms should be able to pick it up."

"I'm on it."

Cyan full-burned the thrusters to gain speed, turning the shuttle away from the planet toward the distant moons. They worked together in silence as he monitored the shuttle's systems for any attempts of a hack and she piloted. The two shuttles followed.

"How do you plan to lose them inside the cluster?"

She took a deep breath. "We're in luck. Look at the weapons inventory. We have hull busters."

"I'm not familiar with them."

"Sorry. About five years ago they invented them on Earth. We're going to drop six of them in our wake when we hit the cluster. I'd drop more but that's all there is. They are a weapon with a four-minute timer once deployed. They blow apart and leave a big debris field of sharp metals designed to breach a hull. That should slow those bastards down or they'll have to fly around the entire cluster to avoid the mess. It will buy us enough time to get out of their radar range to lose them."

Krell stared at her. "I'm proud of you."

She wasn't sure what to say but her chest tightened over the compliment. "Thanks. I feel the same way when it comes to you."

His gaze drifted away. "I put you in danger. I should have left you on Garden where you would have been safe."

Irritation flashed through her. "That's bullshit. They would have tortured the location of your planet from at least one of you if those metal heads had captured your people. They would have gone there next."

His silence wasn't exactly an agreement but she let it slide. They hit the sector of small moons and she released the six weapons, leaving them in their wake, and changed direction, steering around the moons until she passed through the cluster.

"Where do we go now?"

Krell hesitated.

It hurt. Cyan released the controls and stood. "Fine. I'm going to go somewhere else. You have the helm since you don't trust me enough to tell me how to reach Garden."

She refused to meet his gaze though she knew he watched her as she spun away and marched toward the lift. He didn't call out to stop her and she hadn't expected him to. Krell only trusted her up to a certain point. It sucked and it hurt her feelings but the important thing was they'd escaped. They'd reach Garden alive.

Krell snarled and took the helm. He wanted to set it to autopilot but couldn't trust it since the Markus Models had previously had control of the shuttle. He needed to monitor it closely to make sure it wasn't programmed to send out any signals to the other androids' shuttles. He should have told Cyan the coordinates to Garden. Trust didn't come easy to him but she'd earned it tenfold.

"I'm an ass," he muttered, wishing he could go after her. He would apologize when she returned.

Part of him wished they didn't have to return to Garden immediately. The idea of spending time alone with Cyan was a pleasant one. The council couldn't issue any orders regarding his female and he wouldn't have to deal with other males wishing to gain Cyan's interest. The moment they reached orbit he'd have to issue a request to meet with them, order Mavo to attend to verify her previous human identity, and argue for her to be given special concessions.

He hoped the council would take Mavo's word that Cyan had once been Emily Pleva. He'd call on Councilman Zorus as well to help sway them to approve his demands to give her human status on Garden despite her body's origins. The male owed him a lot of favors and he'd call in every one to prevent Cyan from having to take other males into their family unit.

She may not even want to stay with me. That haunting thought made him snarl. His fingers wrapped around the controls tighter at the idea of losing her. He had to make it right with her and indecision tore at him again. He wanted to seek her out and apologize. He always seemed to screw up when it came to her. He'd spent too many years alone, didn't have friends for a reason, and he'd lost his ability to communicate well.

I need to try harder, he admitted. *I need to tell her how much she means to me.*

* * * * *

Hours had passed and Cyan hadn't returned. It worried Krell but internal sensors confirmed that she remained on the lower deck in the crew sleeping quarters and he hoped she at least rested well.

The coms alerted him to a signal and he opened a channel to listen. Silence greeted him but then a soft beep sounded.

He smiled, recognizing the signal for what it was. "This is Krell. I am piloting the Genesis Four."

The com remained silent for a moment. "Prove it."

246

He flat-out grinned. "You're an asshole for nearly dumping my female onto her ass just because she proved you are incompetent at reading her, Gene." He paused. "Where are you hiding?" His gaze drifted over the radar, impressed with the *Bridden*'s abilities to cloak, avoiding being detected easily by sensors.

"What happened to the Markus Models?"

"Cyan killed them and we left their remains on the planet surface."

"All of them?"

"The eight Models who were previously on this shuttle have been deactivated. We encountered two more shuttles when we broke the surface of the hostile planet but she lost them."

"Continue on. We're in range." A blip suddenly showed on the radar screen, but only for a second, and Krell grinned. The other shuttle flew portside, pacing him, and had purposely revealed its location.

"What is the status of the *Vontage*?"

"Safe and ahead of us. We backtracked, searching for you and to verify it wasn't a trap when we received your original transmission that you were traveling in the attack shuttle. We didn't believe it."

"Now you have verification."

Mission accomplished on getting the Vontage *home.* A sense of peace hit Krell. He'd done his job and now he just needed to convince Cyan to keep him as her primary and only male. His body tensed. He'd do that after he convinced the council to revoke her cyborg female status and change it to give her human rights.

* * * * *

Cyan stared at the ceiling of the crew cabin. She'd napped a little but nightmares had plagued her. She'd probably have them for a while after her encounter with the Markus Models. The damn things would continue to search for cyborgs but she'd do her best to make sure they never captured any. She'd share all her information about them with Krell and make sure they carried weapons that would be effective. He might not trust her completely but she'd make him listen.

She was in love with a guy who might never fully believe what she said. He was stubborn and could make her angry more than anyone else ever had but he was worth the trouble. A smile curved her lips. Convincing him could be fun. The memories of making up after they argued made her climb off the bunk.

She left the crew cabin and found the kitchen. The Markus Models needed to sustain the organic parts of their bodies but the food stores were nearly depleted. She managed to put two plates together and hoped they weren't in for a long trip. They'd starve.

Krell turned his head when she entered the piloting section of the shuttle. His dark gaze widened slightly at the sight of the trays she carried. She slowly advanced toward him.

"I thought you might be hungry."

"I am." He turned to face her. "I apologize."

That brought her to a halt. She hesitated before she approached, took the second seat, and handed over a tray of food. "Thank you. What is the apology for?"

248

"I do trust you. It is just not easy for me to do."

Her body relaxed. "That means a lot, Krell. Really."

He accepted the food, glanced at it, but didn't show a grimace. Cyan wanted to do it for him. The pickings were slim.

"It seems the Markus Models didn't restock food. We're kind of screwed in that department pretty soon. They don't need to eat as much as we do and they can go longer periods of time without nourishment. This was the best of what was left."

"We'll reach Garden soon. We've advanced on the *Vontage* but we're keeping back enough to give them cover in case they find trouble on the return trip. This is the faster shuttle yet we are taking the rear position." He used his head to indicate the sensors.

Cyan glanced at them, seeing a faint blip on the radar. They were a good hour behind it at least. "That's her? Where's the *Bridden*?"

"Cloaked but present. It is off our portside."

Cyan ate, her thoughts on returning to Garden and what that would mean for her and Krell. She glanced up when she finished to find him staring at her. "What?"

"Would you enjoy flying us the rest of the way to Garden? We're planning on docking to the *Vontage* when we reach orbit. A team is going to sweep this shuttle first before it's taken to the surface and they will replace the onboard computers to make certain we don't have any surprises in the future if they programmed them to send a distress signal or broadcast to the androids. We'll board the *Bridden* and it will return us to the surface."

249

He was offering her an olive branch of sorts and she took it. "I'd love to." She smiled. Krell stood, took both their trays and allowed her to fly the Genesis Four shuttle. Cyan spent the rest of the flight in comfortable silence with him.

Chapter Fourteen

"Home sweet home," Cyan chuckled, dropped her bag inside Krell's door and turned her head to peer up at him.

He dropped his own bag and moved out of the way so the door could close behind him. He hesitated. "We need to talk."

Her heart dropped. "That's never good to hear a man say."

That drew a frown from him. "I don't understand."

"Are you breaking up with me?" She used a teasing tone but inside she winced, expecting painful words to come out of his mouth. She hoped that wasn't the case.

"No." He took a step forward, gripped her arms and yanked her against his body to face him. "I'm your primary male and you're my female. We're joined in a family unit and I do not wish to dissolve it."

She could breathe easier. "Okay. What do you want to talk about?" Her hands flattened on his chest.

"I'm requesting an immediate meeting with the council. Mavo has verified your claims and therefore I'm insisting they issue you a new status."

"English?"

"You were once fully human, you saved cyborgs from Earth captivity, and you deserve special concessions. I do not wish for males coming after you to gain your interest in hopes of them joining our family unit."

"That was clear enough."

"Will you protest my right to be with you?"

"I don't understand."

He leaned down a little closer. "We've had our disagreements but I wish for you to remain with me, Cyan. You could protest our joining, ask the council to give you to another male, but I don't want that to happen." He took a deep breath. "I value you greatly and wish you to know I would protest losing you. I'd battle the entire council if they attempt to assign you to another male. I wish to be your primary and only male on a permanent basis."

Her fingers traced the material of his shirt and she stared at it for a few seconds before lifting her gaze. "Why?"

The baffled look on his face wasn't amusing but it was cute. "Why?"

"Why do you want to keep me?"

"I find you attractive."

She hid her wince.

"You're intelligent, creative and mine." He blew out a frustrated breath. "I want to keep you. I feel things with you that I never have experienced before."

That perked her up. "What kind of feelings?"

"You want me to evaluate them and give you descriptions?"

"It doesn't sound real romantic put that way." Her hands slid up to his shoulders and her chin lifted higher. "You could show me what you feel."

Passion flared in his gaze and Cyan grinned. Krell lowered his head to kiss her but the door chimed. They both groaned and she released him. He eased away from her and turned, his palm slamming hard over the pad next to them. The doors slid open to reveal a large group of people in the hallway.

"No," Krell hissed.

Cyan was at a loss for words. Mavo and Deviant stood in front of some of the councilmen she'd met at Medical. There had to be ten or more of them and she was glad to see her friend but confused by his angry expression as he glared at Krell. Mavo dropped his gaze to seek her out.

"I've come for you," Mavo informed her softly. "You are no longer joined in a family unit with Krell. My son and I have the support of the council to take you away from him."

"What?" Surprise rolled through her.

"I petitioned the council and they agree that you shouldn't have been assigned to any male. I spoke to my female and while she wasn't happy, she understands my association with you. You are officially considered my daughter, under my protection and that of my son Deviant. We've come to take you to my home."

Krell suddenly surged forward, grabbed Mavo by the front of his shirt and the council members gasped. They scrambled to get out of the way as both men were propelled into the hallway. Cyan was so stunned she couldn't move until Mavo's back hit the wall and Krell roared out.

"She's mine and you had no authority."

253

Mavo gripped his hands. "You had no right to hide the news that she'd been returned to us and to keep her. Put me down and stop this immediately."

Deviant stepped into Krell's home and held out his hand. "Come with me and my father, Cyan."

She stared at the unusually dark-skinned cyborg, letting it sink in that he was Mavo's son. "No."

"You'll be safe. My father and mother have adopted you, in a sense, and you'll be safe living in my father's home."

She gaped at him.

"You want her, Deviant." Krell dropped Mavo, spun, glared at the other cyborg and growled. "Don't deny it."

Deviant shrugged. "I believe I know much about her after all my father's stories. I've heard about her my entire life."

Jazel, the female council woman with the pale hair, shoved the men out of her way. "Enough. This is unacceptable. We are better than behaving as if we're poorly trained humans. What is next? A fight with fists?" She turned her head to peer at Cyan. "You've been released from your family unit, your status has been changed to human regardless of your enhanced body, and Mavo has claimed you as his daughter. You may leave with your father."

Cyan threw up her hands. "Wait a damn minute. Doesn't anyone care what I want?"

"No," Krell snarled. "They do not."

Her gaze landed on Mavo. "We need to talk." She glanced at Krell. "Alone."

Anger tightened his features. "I knew you would choose him." Pain flashed across his handsome features, he didn't even attempt to hide it, and then he stormed down the hallway out of sight.

Mavo smoothed his wrinkled uniform and approached her. "It will be fine, E—" He paused. "Cyan."

She reached out, gripped his arm, pulled him inside Krell's home and shot Deviant a glare. "Get out."

"My father—"

"Out!" She kept hold of Mavo and used her finger to point. "Leave."

Deviant wasn't happy but stepped out into the hallway. Cyan tugged Mavo inside until the door slid shut to afford them some privacy. She realized it probably pissed off the council but she didn't care. She released Mavo and faced him, her hands gripping her hips.

"Why did you do that?"

He appeared confused. "I'm saving you."

"From Krell?"

"Yes." His green eyes narrowed. "He was irrational, threatened to kill me, and prevented me from talking to you. You've found me and I mean to protect you."

"From Krell?"

"Yes."

"Damn." She sighed, staring up at him. "Did you think you might want to ask me first? You know how I hate people doing that crap. How many times did you used to listen to me bitch about how everyone would always make decisions for me in the ruse of protecting me?"

"E—" He groaned. "I'm trying to adjust to your new name. I don't want to harm you again by saying the other one."

"I appreciate that. The stabbing pain to my head sucks. Just talk to me without using names. You'll adjust in time."

"Fine. Krell isn't known for his ability to get along with others and he's acting irrational when it comes to you. I imagined you would be relieved to be free of him. We can finally be together."

"You're married."

He frowned. "Yes. I adopted you."

"I'm an adult. That's kind of weird."

"I always thought of you as a daughter."

Ouch. Good thing I'm not infatuated with him anymore or that would really hurt instead of just sting a tiny bit. She hesitated.

"I failed you once when I abandoned you on Earth. I should have ignored your reasoning and carried you away."

"I would have died."

"I read the reports the council created on you as soon as we contacted Garden." Rage darkened his features. "You did die. That's how you ended up changed."

"True, but you're missing the point. I'm still here because I stayed on Earth and this happened. I hated it at first. I was in shock after I woke, but it didn't totally suck. The height thing gets to me but I adjusted and grew into being a new person. It's me now. I'm not the same person and as much as I appreciate you trying to protect me, you're not."

"No one will tell you who to be with."

"My point exactly. It's my choice and no one asked me if I wanted to leave Krell."

Some of his anger faded. "You care for him?"

"Duh. Yes. We have our problems but we're trying to work through them."

Mavo's features paled slightly. "I've made things worse. I'm so sorry."

"You didn't know. You totally get an A for effort though. I appreciate that. It's why I'm not yelling."

A smile tugged at his lips. "I've missed you."

She smiled back and stepped into him, wrapped her arms around his waist and hugged him tightly. "I missed you too."

His strong arms wrapped around her and he placed a kiss on the top of her head. "I was hoping that you'd be attracted to my son. He's very similar to me." He chuckled. "I want the best for you."

She laughed. "Still as conceited as ever."

"Still as mouthy as ever."

"Some things never change."

He held her tighter. "You mean the world to me." His voice grew gruff. "Leaving you behind destroyed me and I've grieved the loss all these years."

"It's a good thing I'm tough to kill and your creator was a genius." She fought back tears. "The new bod is pretty kickass and it was for the best. No more grieving allowed for a live person."

He chuckled. "You're officially my daughter. I insist on keeping that ruling in place."

"Awesome. I'm not calling you Daddy though. I'd need therapy."

He pulled back a little to give her a confused look. "Why?"

"I had a crush on you once."

His lips parted in surprise.

"Don't worry. I'm so over it. We're good."

"I didn't realize."

"It doesn't matter. What does is that Krell took off and I'm in love with him."

"I'll find him and bring him back." Mavo released her. "I'll fix this. I'll petition the council to reinstate your family unit immediately."

She shook her head. "Don't. If Krell wants me, he can get the paperwork done to reinstate our marriage. I don't want someone telling us how to live without each of us having a say in it first, this time around. I'm not leaving him unless he asks me to."

"He's completely irrational where you are concerned." Mavo grinned. "There's no paperwork on Garden. It's all electronics. We do hold meetings. You're irresistible and he never stood a chance. I should have seen through his rage to the reason behind it. He stopped me from taking you aboard the *Vontage* because he didn't want the two of you parted. He loves you."

"I hope so." She crossed her fingers. "Now could you leave and take the circus outside with you? I doubt he'll return until they are gone."

Mavo chuckled. "Done on the condition that you see me often. We're family."

"Try to keep me away. I've got to meet this wife of yours. She must be something to have landed you."

His smile faded. "It's not a love match but we get along well and she's given me two sons. I was her fourth addition into her family unit and I'm not her primary male."

"I'm sorry."

He shrugged. "Things are what they must be for our survival. They aren't ideal but we're striving to make them better. We're happier now than we ever were on Earth."

"You know I'm going to raise hell for things to change."

"I look forward to it." He laughed. "I almost feel sorry for the council after seeing what you used to do to your fath— When you disagreed with how things were run. Remember that you love me."

"Remember to ask me first next time you want to do what is best for me and we'll be good. Otherwise I'll reprogram something of yours to go haywire."

Mavo laughed. "I've missed you."

"Ditto. Go, and take them with you. I've got the grim cyborg to talk to."

"I'd tell you good luck but you won't need it. You're the most determined female I've ever met. He doesn't stand a chance."

Cyan watched Mavo open the door and leave. She turned and walked through Krell's home, wondering how long he'd be gone. Time might be a good thing considering she had some plotting to do.

She never wanted to return to Earth. She didn't have any ties there. The people she loved were on Garden. They were her family now. She belonged with the cyborgs and to one in particular.

* * * * *

Krell wandered aimlessly through the streets, attempting to think but hurt and anger made it nearly impossible. He'd been betrayed by his best friend, a male he considered a brother, who had taken his female. Cyan had an attachment to Mavo and they had a history.

His teeth ground together. It had taken Mavo under a minute to identify Cyan as Emily Pleva, the daughter of their creator and the savior of cyborgs. He'd trusted her instantly, unlike Krell. She had every reason to wish to leave with Mavo and to live in his home.

Krell's hands fisted. *Deviant, that devious cyborg, wants Cyan bad.* He growled, drawing attention from passing cyborgs, but ignored them all. Loss and jealousy battled inside his mind as he wandered the streets.

He regretted not having the time to talk to Cyan before the council and his friends had arrived at his door. He should have ignored it but he'd had

260

no way of knowing they'd act so quickly to remove her from his home. For once he had something, someone, to live for. He'd learned to care and to feel happiness. The cold reserve he always carried had slipped away to admit the sexy and mouthy little female instead.

He stopped walking and spun around on his booted heel. He wasn't going to allow her to go without a fight. A plan formed in his head as he hurried home. He'd grab a bag, go after Cyan and steal a shuttle. He just needed a few days with her to convince her that he was the male for her.

She'd argue and perhaps fight with him physically when he kidnapped her but a smile played at his lips as he considered that concept. He enjoyed making up with Cyan. She'd get over her temper soon enough. They had chemistry and feelings were involved.

The hallway in front of his door had emptied and his rage returned. Cyan had been taken and there wasn't a reason anyone would stick around his home any longer. They had gotten the one thing they wanted. He unlocked the door, stormed inside and headed for his bedroom to grab weapons from his closet.

He may have to fight his way to one of the shuttles if an alarm was triggered when he broke into Mavo's home to retrieve Cyan. It wouldn't matter. They wouldn't risk shooting at him with her over his shoulder. He'd move swiftly, steal a shuttle and blast off from the planet. He'd figure out a way to lose whatever ships they sent after him. He could hide for a few days to give him the needed time to make Cyan see they belonged together.

He marched into his bedroom and headed quickly for the closet, but something caught his attention, jerking him to a halt. Cyan sat on his bed staring at him silently. Her boots were removed, along with her pants, and her naked, pale legs were crossed. She wore one of his shirts, the only item she appeared to have on, and her hair had been unbraided to fall in a black mass over her shoulders onto his bedding. The blue of her eyes drew him in as he held his breath before stumbling a step toward her.

"It took you long enough to come home. What did you do? Walk the entire city?" Her dark eyebrows arched and her lips curved downward. "I thought I was going to have to send a search party after you but didn't know who to call."

"Cyan?" His gruff voice came out sounding harsh and he regretted it but he was shocked to find her there.

"Who else? Do I look like the maid? Strike that. I'm not into cleaning and I'm not exactly dressed for it either unless you want to see me bend over to scrub the floor just to flash my ass at you." She suddenly grinned. "That sounds kinky and I might consider it."

He took another step closer, stunned that she was really there, confused too, but happy. "You didn't leave?"

"Duh. Hello!" She gripped her shapely inner thighs and leaned in his direction. "Are you all right? You look a little pale."

"I'm...baffled."

"You look it." Her grin widened. "Why don't you take a seat? I thought we should talk."

His heart raced and dread tensed his body. "You stayed to say goodbye to me?"

"Sit." She released her thigh and pointed to the mattress next to her. "I'm starting to get a crick in my neck from staring up at you. Damn, you're tall."

Krell inched closer and sat on the edge of the bed, turned to face her and realized he had an opportunity to convince her to stay. He might not have much time, Mavo and Deviant would return for her, but for now they were alone. Worst-case scenario, he'd toss her over his shoulder, grab what he needed and take her off the planet if she refused to consider remaining with him.

"Cyan—"

Cyan launched at Krell and straddled his lap, cutting off his words. She cupped his face, couldn't miss the shock at her swift actions, and she studied his beautiful eyes. "Here's where we're at. The council disbanded, divorced us, or whatever they call it." She shrugged. "Mavo adopted me as his daughter. That's disturbing yet sweet in a kind of creepy way, considering I used to fantasize about him. That puts a whole new spin on that sex-daddy thing." She shivered. "I'm so not into that. Ewww."

It amused her when Krell's eyes widened with shock and he just gaped at her. She refrained from laughing, her fingers traced his scars softly and she scooted higher up his thighs until they were chest to chest. She liked being on his lap since it helped them even out their heights.

"I'm really tired of people telling me how to live. Aren't you? We have a clean slate now. We're both free to do what we want."

He suddenly gripped her hips, yanking her tighter against his groin, and her eyebrows lifted when she felt more than his thighs under her. The smile returned, knowing how she affected him. He was more than happy to see her—he was aroused, hard, and obviously turned-on.

"I want you, Cyan. Don't leave me. I know that other males would probably be easier to live with and I'm aware of my flaws but I will work on them."

"What flaws?" Her fingers traced his scars again. "I think you're incredibly hot, Krell. You're strong, brave, smart and very sexy."

He softly growled and it turned her on more. There was something untamed and wild about him when he did it, so far from the reserved guy he tried to be.

"And then there's that. I love when you make those noises and let some of that iron control of yours go." She spread her thighs wider, snugly fitting her pussy over the hard length of his cock, trapped in his pants, and slid her hands around his neck until their lips nearly touched. "There's not a damn thing wrong with you in my book."

"I do have flaws."

"Who doesn't? I happen to have a few myself. I'm so not a morning person sometimes. I'm actually kind of scary." She smiled to soften the words. "And I speak bad English, according to you."

"I think it's endearing."

Her heart melted. "Really?"

"Yes." He held her tighter. "I don't want to lose you, Cyan. I need you. I wanted to tell you that and make you understand that you are deeply valued by me."

"I'm looking for more than value here." She bit her lip. "Have you ever loved anyone before? Do you think it's possible for you to one day fall in love with me?"

His gaze narrowed. "Not one day."

It hurt and she lowered her gaze, tried to lean away from his body, but he suddenly fisted a handful of her hair at the base of her neck to keep her in place. She stared at him in surprise.

"I love you, Cyan Eous. It's not going to come to pass one day because it has already occurred. I believe it happened the moment you walked up to me inside the interrogation cell and touched me. You made me feel with your light caress, the way you pressed against me and the look in your eyes when I stared into them."

"I think that was sexual attraction."

"You're not my female type but you've become it." His hold on her hair loosened. "It was deeper than that. You saw me and not just the scars. I didn't terrify you or repulse you. I was a male." He released her hair and cupped her face. "You make me feel happy to be in your presence and fear at the same time that you may one day leave me. You anger me but I enjoy arguing with you. I'm alive with you and you make everything possible for me. I may not have experienced love before but I'm an analyst." His lips curved upward into a smile. "I'm smart enough to figure out what I'm feeling. I am in love and I believe you love me as well. You could have left but you are here, wearing my shirt, on my bed, and you had a choice."

Tears filled her eyes. "I love you too, Krell. I don't want to leave. This is where I belong, with you, and it's the only place I want to be."

"I'll never let you go and I'll never share you with other males." He hesitated, his smile gone, and anger darkened his eyes. "The idea makes me feel rage thinking about them baring your body, getting to know you, and you touching them. You're mine. I want to be your primary and only male."

"I told you I'm not into that multi-partner thing. Ewww. You're more than enough for me and I don't want anyone else. The council will be very sorry if they try to pull that cyborg, messed-up law bullshit on us. I can be a real bitch and I—"

Krell's mouth covered hers and she moaned against his kiss. His tongue delved inside to tease her with light caresses that left her panting when he finally pulled away. He stared into her eyes.

"I do remember some things about humans."

"Okay. Would that be how to annoy someone when they want to have sex and you stop instead?"

He chuckled and lifted her off his lap, despite her protest. He set her on the edge of the bed and he slid to the floor. He knelt before her and she hoped he was about to get kinky. She longed for him to turn her around and do it doggy style. Her body ached for him but instead he took her hand, lifted it to his lips, and pressed a kiss to the back of it. His dark gaze locked with hers while he kept hold of her.

"Cyan Eous, will you marry me? I promise to love, honor and cherish you. I will protect you with my life, give you my alliance above all others, including the council and other cyborgs, and swear loyalty to you for as long as I draw breath. I will put your needs above my own, always attempt to make certain you are happy, and I—"

She yanked him off balance, using his hold on the hand he clutched, and took him to the floor by launching her body against his. Krell landed flat on his back with her straddling his lap. She leaned over him, her hair falling forward to curtain around them, and laughed.

"You had me at 'will you marry me'. Yes!"

He chuckled. "You're very strong."

"People always underestimate me."

He surprised her by bucking his hips, released her hand he still held, and rolled them. Her back hit the floor and the sexy cyborg pinned her tightly. He grinned as he yanked her arms over her head and snugly cradled his hips into the vee of her thighs. His cock pressed firmly against her clit, rubbed as he wiggled against her to get more comfortable, and she softly moaned.

"Will you ever allow me to finish a sentence?"

"Probably not." She wrapped her legs around his hips. "Will you ever stop teasing me and shut up? Less talk, more clothes off."

He grinned. "There is so much I love about you."

"There'd be so much more of you to love if you'd take off the clothes."

"I want a joining ceremony and we'll share markings."

"What does that mean? Could you speak English I can understand?"

He released her arms and lifted up. "Tear my shirt off."

Cyan grabbed the material, more than happy to comply. She had no problems helping him out of his clothes. She loved to bare every inch of him. The sound was loud as she shredded it from his body. He held still to allow her to do it and she freed his upper body and tossed the destroyed shirt away. Her hands flattened on his impressive, muscular chest and slid downward to open the front of his pants. He suddenly lowered, trapping her hands between their stomachs.

"Our males tattoo their names and who we are in our cyborg language across our arms and shoulders. I had enough scars to carry and never wanted more markings. That has changed with you." He braced one arm to hold his weight, used his hand to brush his outer arm with his fingertips and trace them upward to his shoulder and across his upper back. "They would be placed along here."

"You created a language? Is it hard to speak? I'm pretty good at learning new ones."

"It's just a written language. We did it to communicate with each other without others being able to understand it. I'll teach it to you." He paused, peering deeply into her eyes. "It would mean a lot to me if you'd carry my name, if we shared the same markings and were matched."

"Have you ever heard of a wedding band? You know, matching rings on our fingers?"

Disappointment flashed across his handsome features. "Yes. I understand. Carrying the markings of another on your body is a hard burden to bear."

It mattered to him, meant a lot, and that mattered to her. He'd carried the scars of his attack by humans, would always have that reminder, but now he wanted to sport something they'd share on their bodies. She got it and it made her heart melt.

"I'd be honored to get matching tattoos with you."

He smiled. "Really?"

"Yes. I just hope they are attractive. You'll be looking at them for a very long time because you're stuck with me for good. I kind of heal fast and hope tattoos take."

"Our bodies take them and so will yours. We use magnetic ink placed under the skin to manipulate the exact patterns we wish. Your skin will tolerate it and the wraps we use will hold it in place while you heal to keep the pattern. The cyborg written language is beautiful to view. I'll have some of the males show you before it is done so you may see it. I'll write out my name to show you what ours will be, exactly."

"Awesome but I'm sure I'll love it. I really don't want a bunch of guys stripping off their shirts in front of me. I'm content to just admire yours once we get them done."

He chuckled. "Awesome."

Cyan laughed. "You know, I'm totally going to be a bad influence on you. You're already picking up my colorful sayings."

"I look forward to it."

"Now can we have sex?" She gripped his shoulders, trying to tug him down. "I want you."

He lowered his chest but instead of kissing her, he stared into her eyes. "I have one more request. You don't have to answer now but I'd appreciate your consideration."

"Okay. What is it?"

He hesitated.

"Just spill it."

"I assume that means you want me to just say what is on my mind."

"Yes." She grinned. "You know what I'm thinking about. Your pants are still on though."

"I would enjoy having a child with you at a future date."

That shocked her.

"I realize there is no need, Mavo had one for me in accordance to cyborg law, but I would hope you would at least consider it. I gave up wanting a lot of things but you make me dream for more. I want to experience everything with you, Cyan. I want to live with you in every way possible, become a true family, and to create a life with you would be amazing."

He's perfect, she admitted, as tears filled her eyes. She blinked them back.

"I'm sorry. I've upset you and that wasn't my intention."

"It's not that. I used to dream about having kids. Every little girl does but I was diagnosed with my illness when I was still playing with dolls. I lost all hope of ever becoming a mother and I figured it would be too dangerous to ever try to have one after my body was switched out. My life was unstable with having to dump identities every fifteen or so years. I didn't want to drag a kid into that mess and being a single parent in the military would have meant I couldn't raise my own child."

"You no longer have to hide who you are and you've got a home now with me. Your dreams can come true too. We can do it together, accomplish anything we wish, and we have a long life ahead of us to share."

She closed her eyes.

"Cyan? You can think about this later."

"Hang on."

He adjusted, lifting up, and gripped her borrowed shirt, tugging it up. Her eyes opened and she arched her back, helping him take it off. He rolled off her, unfastened his pants and kicked at his boots to get them off. Cyan laughed, sat up, and helped him strip. Krell stood, reached down and hauled her to her feet.

"The bed would be more comfortable."

She met his gaze. "I turned it off."

"Turned what off?" He wrapped an arm around her waist, drawing him into his embrace and surprised her by lifting her up. He walked them both to the bed, turned and sat, putting her on his lap, facing him.

"My implant. You know, the one that controls my ovaries so I don't ovulate. It might take a while to get pregnant but that means we'll need to try often." She grinned. "A lot. All the time." She leaned closer until she

271

trapped his stiff cock between their bellies, her lips brushing his. "You definitely feel up for it."

A soft growl rumbled from the back of his throat. "I'm your male."

"Yes, you are. I'm your female, who really wants you, baby. Make me happy."

"That's my main priority and I aim to please you."

He kissed her, his arms wrapped around her, and pulled her against him tighter. Cyan moaned, using her fingernails to rake his skin. She loved to touch him, just loved everything about him.

He slid his hands down to cup her ass, urged her to lift up, and she did it, breaking the kiss. Their gazes held as she reached between them, gripped the shaft of his cock and stroked him.

"Take me, Cyan."

She wiggled her pussy over the crown of his cock, rubbed back and forth just enough to spike their desire a little higher. She moaned. "Your job is to please me but my job is going to be taunting you a little. You made me wait. It's only fair."

A growl tore from his throat and he surprised her by suddenly rolling them over. He pinned her under him and began to enter her body slowly. "I never promised to be fair." He winked. "I promised to love and cherish you. I plan to do that now."

She would have laughed but Krell took possession of her mouth, kissing her until she couldn't think.

Joy and happiness filled Krell. Cyan was his to keep and love. A little guilt ate at him for not informing her about the status of his inactive sperm but he'd tell her later, after he made a quick trip to Medical to get the shot that would make it viable. Her fingernails digging into his skin drove his passion higher and the guilt fled to be replaced by pure need.

She'd forgive him for waiting to tell her, guessing she'd be angrier if he pulled away from her body, and no way was he about to do that. Not even an invasion of their planet would drag him away from her before he made love to his Cyan.

He broke the kiss, the desire to watch her lovely features a need he refused to ignore. Passion-kissed lips gasped when he lifted up to stare at her. He rolled his hips, finding the spot that made her cry out his name, and his cock hammered her.

Her vaginal muscles clenched around him. The sensation made his balls draw up tight and he fought back the climax that threatened. Not without her. That promise kept his passion in check.

"Krell!"

Her pleading tone told him what she needed. He shifted his body just enough to brace his weight on one arm and slide his hand between their bodies. He pressed his thumb to her clit. Her eyes narrowed, her moans grew louder and he rubbed the bundle of nerves that would help her come. He fucked her faster, drove into her deeper and the muscles gripping his cock tightened even more.

Heaven, he decided. *That should be Cyan's name.* Her fingernails clawed at his back, the bite of pain sending him into a haze of bliss while

273

torturing him at the same time. He knew he couldn't hold back any longer but he didn't need to. Cyan threw her head back, screamed his name, and her pussy seized as she hit the pinnacle of her pleasure.

Krell roared out, ecstasy blinding him, and emptied his seed deep into her hot, tight body, pinned under his. He shivered, jerked his hand from between them, and rolled over, dragging her with him. She sprawled over his chest and he hugged her tightly.

I'll never let her go. This is where she belongs. With me.

31488085R00160

Printed in Great Britain
by Amazon